QUARRY ROAD

QUARRY ROAD

A.R. DISPALDO

CUTTING EDGE

ISBN-13: 978-1-954840-92-8

Published by
Cutting Edge Books
PO Box 8212
Calabasas, CA 91372
www.cuttingedgebooks.com

CHAPTER ONE

JOE CARATO awoke late on Sunday morning. He scratched his broad, hairy chest and wished to God he were dead. His head wanted to take off and float away. There was something flying around in his stomach. But there was something else about this particular morning after. Something new had been added. He sniffed hard through a battered nose, smashed many years before. The air was fragrant with coffee, bacon and eggs.

This, he thought, is the best damned hangover I ever had. Don't remember waking up like this since Fanny left. He heard cups and saucers being set on the kitchen table. Then the tinkle of forks and spoons. Bacon and eggs made sizzling, popping sounds. And it all made Joe Carato feel somewhat better despite pounding his head.

"Hey! Who the hell's in there?" he yelled into the kitchen. It was a moment before a face appeared in the doorway. Joe shook his head vigorously.

"I can't be awake," he muttered to himself. He slapped hard at his face. It made him blink. Still the beautiful image did not disappear. Instead, more of it came into view, partly covered with a slip.

He stared unbelievingly. "Who—are you?"

The lovely face flashed a tiny apologetic smile. "I am Teresa." There was a faint, very slight accent. But it seemed natural and went well with her large soft brown eyes and the dark luxurious hair reaching to her shoulders.

Suddenly, Joe was conscious of his huge hairy nakedness. He tried to cover up his chest. This crazy kid he told himself is young enough to be my daughter. Maybe even young enough to be jail-bait.

He asked, "Where'd you come from, kid, and what the hell are you doing here?"

"You picked me up in town last night and you brought me back with you in the car." Her explanation was as simple as that. His eyes wandered down the length of her slight body. Her thinness only accentuated the ample bosom that swelled against the cheap cloth. He stared hard where the slip was pulled taut across her hips and thighs.

"Say—" he hesitated—"did you—did I—"

She stared with wide questioning eyes.

"Where did you sleep?" he finally blurted out.

"In the bed. You made me get in with you," she apologized.

Now the beads of perspiration flowed freely down his face. "Did I—did I do anything?" It was almost a whisper.

"No." She looked at him frankly. "You were drunk."

A fleeting smile touched his mouth. Hell, he sure wasn't drunk now.

"Come here," he whispered, his voice growing husky.

"The eggs will burn."

"To hell with the eggs."

"Aren't you hungry?"

"No, I'm not hungry. Come here."

"Very well, then. I will come. Please wait a moment."

She disappeared into the kitchen. The sizzling of the bacon and eggs stopped. She reappeared through the doorway. "You are sure that you do not want to eat first?"

Joe felt the throbbing in his temples. His mouth refused to form words. He shook his head.

"Very well, then." Her voice was thin, like a child's.

She removed her slip and laid it carefully over a chair. Joe's gasp was audible in the small room as she freed her firm heavy breasts. She laid the bra on the slip. She stepped out of her panties and left the tiny wisp of cloth lying on the floor.

Do I please you, her eyes asked him.

"You're beautiful." He answered her unspoken question.

She came slowly to the bed. The sheet rustled. She stared, fascinated. The room was still, and dim with the shades down. She moistened her lip, grown dry. Then, like an obedient child, she got into the bed. "I will make you happy," she whispered. She kissed him full on the mouth, forcing it open.

Joe's arms had remained at his side as though paralyzed. But only for a moment. He rolled over carrying her with him, her body against his. He found her mouth again in a hard, brutal kiss. There was only a tiny cry from the girl as Joe's hulking body crushed her savagely.

It was hot that morning. With the shades down, it was stifling. Outside, the Colella family was readying for church, the children laughing and screaming at each other. Mrs. Colella was yelling first at one, then at another not to get their Sunday best all dirtied up. Giovanni Colella yelled at his wife not to make so much noise. Finally, they left and it was quiet once more on this hot Sunday morning when Teresa came to live with Joe Carato.

CHAPTER TWO

QUARRY ROAD was just exactly what the name implied. It was an unpaved road leading from the quarry that employed all the road's residents. There were twelve residents, including one fourteen-year-old boy who worked down in the pits after school.

Some years back, the tiny frame bungalows had been built as a development. They had been shiny and gay with paint, then. It had turned out a poor investment for the builder, the ground being much too rocky for excavating. So he had sold the remaining parcel of ground surrounding the little community.

A Mr. Cavallo had begun to work the ground getting out the rocks which were in great demand. There had been some half-hearted opposition from the occupants at first. But when they saw they were waging a losing battle, they began to move out. Cavallo went into full production, taking out the great rocks and small stones. Even the earth that came out was used as refill.

As the original occupants moved out, Mr. Cavallo bought the houses and rented them to his employees. Now, the twelve homes housed all the men who worked the quarry and their families. At best, the houses were now dull and gray and broken down. They were all overcrowded—most of the families swelling to six or seven through the years—in houses built to hold four.

Joe Carato's house was no different. With the disappearance of his wife, it too had gone into a state of abandonment. But at least Joe had plenty of room. He lived alone in the house—since the night the people of the Road had been awakened in the wee hours. Joe Carato had come home from one of his frequent drunken sprees and had been met on the tiny porch by his wife. It had been quite a show for the erstwhile quiet and weary community. The next day, Joe's wife had left while he was at work, a battered suitcase carrying all of her worldly belongings. She had never been seen or heard from since.

On the end of the road, away from the quarry, stood the only store. It, like the other buildings, was small. An addition had been added later to house the store area. And it was a degree better kept than the others. In it, Mrs. Giambra stocked the necessities needed by the community. One could purchase most anything from patent medicines to shoes; meats of a questionable grade to a variety of canned foods. It was a general store and Mrs. Giambra reigned as the center of communications.

Mrs. Colella, Joe's next door neighbor, was dispensing vital information at the moment. She was a large-boned woman in her early forties. Hard work and a large family kept her from getting round and fat. She spoke with an accent as did most of the Italian immigrants who settled here, occasionally interjecting a flowering word or phrase from the homeland.

"Yes, Mrs. Giambra. I saw him come home with her." Every one called her "Mrs. Giambra." "It was Saturday night and he was singing at the top of his big mouth. And that girl, she was no bigger than my little twelve-year daughter. She was helping him up the steps. It is a wonder that he did not get killed in an accident. He was so drunk."

Mrs. Giambra was more interested in the squalid side. "Perhaps they are married?"

"I saw her once in the backyard—and I did not see a ring. She is always wearing the same dress. I do not think she has any other. Joe Carato probably picked her up in town. She moved in with him just like that."

"I hear that she is very pretty." Mrs. Giambra was far from being a good-looking woman. Since her husband had been killed in the quarry, she had openly made advances to Joe Carato. There had been rumors that she had slept with him several times. Joe had neither admitted nor denied it.

"I did not see her face very good—but she has a nice figure." Mrs. Colella threw the barb directly at Mrs. Giambra, and thrilled when she saw her wince. "She is so tiny. And Joe is so big. I thought surely he would cause her much pain. But I guess that type could manage six men like Joe. Is it not so, Mrs. Giambra?"

"Perhaps you are right. But then, how could I know? I do not know Joe Carato that well."

Mrs. Colella laughed to herself, remembering the rumors. "No. Of course you would not know, Mrs. Giambra. I must admit, however, she does keep Joe in. He never goes out with my Giovanni any more."

Mrs. Giambra, feeling the bitter pangs of jealousy as the Colella woman had intended, wanted to terminate the conversation. "Joe will get over it. That will be a dollar and thirty-four cents." She took a cheap copy book from a shelf, opened to the "Colella" page and proceeded to enter the sale.

On Friday night the bill would be settled, and she would cross out the page and start a new one for the Colella family. Practically every family on Quarry Road was indebted to Mrs. Giambra throughout the week—to be settled on pay-day.

Mrs. Colella left, and Mrs. Giambra thumbed idly through the book. She came to an entry for Jake Malancuni. It was over a year old, and still hadn't been settled. Spaced in irregular monthly intervals were new entries. The last one being almost a month back. It was for seventy-five cents. There were eleven such sales and each one represented a bottle of wine.

She would have to see Mr. Malancuni and make him pay his bill. She made a short notation on the bottom of the page.

CHAPTER THREE

IT HADN'T taken Joe Carato long to learn that Teresa was an extremely passionate young animal. Till late afternoon of that first day her passion had been insatiable. Joe had felt as though he had been dragged through the quarry grounds. He had lain in bed, soaking in perspiration while she had gotten up and fried more bacon and eggs.

The smell of coffee permeated the still room. The Colella family had long ago returned from church, and the quiet Sunday afternoon was shattered by their screaming, crying brood.

Teresa called him finally in her soft voice. He staggered up and ate ravenously. She watched him anxiously with her eyes, too big for her tiny face. When he finished, she sat opposite him. She looked at him with fearful apprehension.

"Do you like me?" she asked.

"You're damned right, Baby," he answered. "Even though you almost broke my back." He laughed at the thought.

Her eyes opened wide. "What do you mean?" she asked innocently.

"I mean back there in bed." Joe grinned.

"I only wished to please you." The girl lowered her eyes.

"And you sure did, Baby. Only, you don't have to please me so much."

"Then can I stay?"

The question startled Joe. The thought that the girl might want to stay had never entered his mind. Usually, they stayed overnight. Sometimes, over a week-end. Then it was finished. He hadn't expected anything more from the girl. Hell, she must be half his age. And she was a damned sight prettier than the run of women he had been used to.

"You mean you want to stay here and live with me?"

"I have no other place to go," she said simply.

Joe stood up and walked over to the window facing the Colella home. It was quiet, outside the house. Apparently, they were having Sunday dinner, always a big event in the Colellas' lives. He did not have to ponder the problem too long, however. He came back to the table, faced the girl. "Sure you can stay. We'll go pick up your stuff and you can move in."

A grateful smile came to Teresa's face. She indicated her dress. "This is all I own."

Joe nodded. "Okay. You've moved in."

She rose to her toes and barely made it to his cheek. She kissed him affectionately. "Oh, Joe," she said. "I knew that you were a kind man when I first saw you. I will try to make you very happy.'"

"Okay, Baby. You see that you do." He gave her a gentle pat on her rear.

She sang happily as she cleared the table and began doing the dishes.

Jake Malancuni was watchman at the quarry pits. A one-room shack with a stove and cot and an old discarded table made up his living quarters. His shack stood at the quarry end of the road. All trucks that entered and left the works were checked and counted by Jake. His other duties were keeping children out of the dangerous quarry area.

Mr. Cavallo had seen Jake's fiery mop of red hair and had called him *Cupirosso,* Italian for Redhead. The name had stuck. Jake was a gnome with long muscled arms that gave him the appearance of a small gorilla. It was his grotesque appearance that kept the children away from the quarry. A mother needed only to tell her children that they would be eaten up by *Il Capirosso* if they would so much as go near the shack, and they would quake with terror.

Redhead puffed on his smelly stogie and lounged before his shack door. The sun beat down unmercifully on the metal canopy in front of the shack, making the air close and suffocating despite the shade.

Here comes that lucky bastard, Joe, he thought, as he saw Joe Carato coming up the road to work. Jake had heard all about Joe s woman. How did Joe rate a young girl like that? One day Jake told himself, he must go into town and find one too. If he wasn't so damned ugly, maybe one of the young girls from up the road would come down to visit him. There was that little Colella girl. She must be twelve or thirteen. She had come within sight of the shack several times, and he had called to her, offering chocolates. She had giggled and run away. Oh, well —Mrs. Giambra was about due to make a collection call. She would have to do for the present.

"Hello, Joe," he bellowed. Although he had been brought over from the old country as a small boy, he had managed to lose his accent. He could only guess his age to be around sixty.

Joe had a big grin for him, as usual. "How are you today, you ugly redheaded bastard?" he called as he went by.

"Hey, come here a minute, Joe."

Joe went over to him. His tee shirt, already soaked with perspiration, showed clearly the mat of black hair. "What the hell you want?" he roared good-naturedly.

"When are you gonna send your girl over to see me?"

"Why you redheaded bastard. You'd scare her so that she'd move right the hell out of here."

"Oh, come on, Joe. I'll pay you good."

Joe grinned. "I'll tell you what, Redhead. When she gets tired of me, you'll be the first one. And for nothing. Okay?"

"Okay, Joe. Don't forget, I'm first."

"Right!" Joe slapped Redhead on the back. He was almost twice as big as the gnome-like man, and the slap almost made Jake gag on his stogie. Joe strode away toward the pit.

Redhead took off his filthy felt hat and scratched his head sadly. "Redhead, you poor fool," he muttered. "Ain't a chance in the world of you getting any of that. Big Joe wouldn't give up a good thing like that without a good fight." He stared at Joe's huge back. "And there ain't anybody around here who's gonna fight him for her, neither." He paused in his reflections. "Unless it's that sonofabitchin' Sam Roma. He's just liable to go sniffing around like the sneaking rat he is." He started to chuckle. "I sure would like to see them two tangle."

He looked toward the row of houses, as he heard the sound of a coming car. It braked, then rolled slowly past Joe Carato's house. It picked up speed again and stopped in a cloud of dust along-side the shack where the redhead lounged.

Redhead jumped up and shuffled clear of the cloud of dust that enveloped the shack. The queer shufflingwalk gave him more of the appearance of an ape than ever. Some of the dust had gotten into his eyes and nose, causing him to cough and sneeze. Tears came to his eyes.

"You sonofabitchin' Sam Roma!"

Sam Roma, slim, handsome, rugged, stood before him. A steady diet of sun had given him a healthy, bronzed suntan. "That'll give you an excuse to take a bath," he shouted above the redhead's swearing.

Down in the quarry pit, the men, getting ready for work, looked up and watched them silently. "Never does he tire of teasing the redhead," muttered one of the men.

"One day, he will receive his just punishment," muttered another. They looked at Joe for comment. If Joe saw or heard the commotion, it was lost upon him. He was busy picking out a pick and shovel.

At the shack, the dust had settled. Sam Roma stared at his car. A layer of gray dust had settled over it.

"Make sure you wash my car better this time. You hear, Redhead?"

The redhead answered under his breath.

Sam Roma paid no attention to the redhead's mumbling. He turned suddenly and strode down the dirt ramp toward the men. In several minutes, another day's work would commence. The men would listen to Sam Roma. They would obey him, even though to a man, they hated his guts. The rocks would be taken out of the ground. The pit would grow wider and deeper until the stone was exhausted. It would take many years, but it was inevitable. And when this pit was done with, they would find another.

Redhead finished dusting himself. He sighed deeply. Some day. Some day, the louse would get his. He had seen Sam Roma's car slow down when it passed Joe Carato's house. Jake knew why, too. Joe's woman. Just as inevitable as the quarry pit would be stripped of it's stone, so it would be with Sam Roma and Joe Carato. They would tangle over the girl. Jake would wait and see. It's all he had to do; wait and see. He sighed as he sat down in the shade.

The sweltering heat in the quarry hole was unbearable at two-thirty in the afternoon. Heat waves bounced and made a distorted pattern on the sharp rocky contours. Heat seared the eyes so that it was almost impossible to keep them open. Sweat poured freely from the bodies of the men and their clothing clung to their bodies.

Joe Carato, grimy with the dust of the quarry, called to Sam Roma. "We're gonna knock off, Sam. It's too hot to work anymore today. Must be over a hundred down here."

Sam Roma looked cool in khaki pants and shirt, with sleeves rolled up. He had just come down into the pit, having been under the shade of a tree up above. "You speaking for yourself, Joe?" he asked.

"Hell no. The guys are about to keel over. We just talked it over and we decided to call it a day."

"You know what Mr. Cavallo said about falling behind in schedule. This order has to be delivered by the fifteenth. And we sure as hell won't do it this way."

"I'm sorry, Sam. It's too damned hot." Joe threw a huge wrecking bar on his shoulders and started to walk up out of the hole. The other men started to pick up their tools.

"Wait a minute, you guys." Sam's voice was icy cold. "Listen to me. Anybody leaves now takes tomorrow off. You want to work tomorrow, you dig until I say you quit."

The men watched Joe. It was up to him. And it put a great burden of decision upon him. He knew that the men all wanted to leave. But he also knew that they couldn't afford to lose a whole day's work. He went back to his spot, and the men resumed working.

Sam's grin turned into a nasty smirk. He wanted to taunt Joe, make a wisecrack about his woman. He decided against it, however. Joe was in too mean a mood.

It was a scant five minutes later when the horn of a car blasted down upon then. The men stopped working as they focused bleary eyes on the top of the ramp. A tall slender blonde, looking entirely too cool in a white skirt and blouse, looked down upon them.

"Oh, Sam," she called.

"Maybe I'll let you quit after all," Sam said quietly to the men. He waved up at the girl and started to walk up the ramp toward her. The men watched expectently as Sam kissed her lightly on the lips. Sam Roma and the blonde spoke for a few moments, then he called down to them:

"Okay, you guys. Might as well take off the rest of the day."

"Thanks for nothing," growled one of the men.

"He sounds like he is a real nice guy in front of the boss' daughter," muttered another.

Joe Carato picked up the wrecking bar once more and trudged out of the pit. The others followed. Before they had reached the top of the long sloping ramp, the girl and Sam had driven off, his car following behind the girl's in a cloud of dust....

When Joe left for work that morning Teresa stared at herself in the mirror. The new dress Joe had bought her looked pretty, and she was glad. She hoped that it would please Joe. She sighed. Joe was so good to her. He bought her nice things and he let her stay in his house. But what was more important, he didn't ask her so many questions.

After that first day together, he had not asked her many questions. Not that she minded him asking her. She would be glad to tell Joe anything about herself that he wanted to know. But she hated answering questions. It was always so confusing. Sometimes it actually hurt her in the head—when she had to think out an answer. If only she could remember more easily. She so wanted to tell Joe everything about herself but everything was so hazy.

She easily remembered her childhood, though. She remembered the dismal little house and the sky that was always cloudy, as though it were about to rain. She remembered the tiny candy store and Schultzy. Everybody called him Schultzy because he was such a nice man. He always gave the children candy.

He had given her candy, too. One day, he had asked her to come to the back of the store so that he could show her a doll. She remembered clearly that she was fourteen and she had told him that she was too old to play with dolls. Then he had told her to come to the back to pick out a box of candy. She had gone into the back room. And when he had put her on the couch, she had cried out that he was wrinkling her freshly ironed dress. He had hurt her, too. Just a little bit, though.

Afterwards, Schultzy had told her that if she said anything to her parents, they would scold her. And she had never told them. She had been angry because he had not given her a box of candy. But he had given her a handfull and told her she could have a box when she came again. Afterwards, when she went to Schultzy's store, she made sure that her dress wasn't just newly ironed. And sure enough, the box of candy was always there. She had liked Schultzy until her family had moved out of the neighborhood.

At the tenement house, where they had two tiny rooms, she remembered the wall paper that kept coming down with part of the plaster. Also that the rooms were always cold and she used to sleep wrapped up in her coat to keep warm. Her mother and rather were always arguing—and, one night, he had not come home. The only thing she remembered about her father was his pretty mustache. She loved to sit on his lap and twirl it round and round. And he used to laugh and pinch her cheeks.

When she was old enough she went to work in a candy factory. She had liked her job very much because the candy reminded her of Schultzy. Every payday, when she brought home her pay, her mother would go out and buy a bottle of whisky. She said that the doctor had told her she needed it for her health.

They had been very happy together. There were no longer any arguments. She used to come home and cook supper for her mother who didn't seem to be getting any better with the whisky that the doctor had prescribed. And one day they took her mother to the hospital. She died several weeks later. They said something about her liver. Teresa had cried very much.

One day, one of the men from the factory had driven her home and had stayed with her for a long time. She had been very happy with him until the night he had slapped her because she wouldn't give him money. She remembered how dark it was outside when she left him asleep. With just the clothing she had on, she went away.

She had met a nice man who had driven her away from Pittsburg. And except for the fact that he had left her asleep in the hotel room, he also had been nice. He left five dollars on the bureau.

Then she had met Joe. He was the nicest of all. He bought her clothing and treated her real nice. And he was so big. Even bigger than Schultzy. She shivered with pleasure. If Joe were only here now, she would show him how much she appreciated him.

She took off her dress, folded it neatly, and put it away in a drawer. She looked at herself in the mirror. Her body had filled out and her skin glowed with a healthy fullness. She cupped her breasts and raised them until they thrust outward in front of her. When she released them, they swung gently. She was proud of her body and glad that she had it to lavish on Joe.

She covered herself with a housecoat. Outside, she heard the car again. She knew that it would slow down when it passed the house. It always did. She went to the window and peeked out. She had never seen such a handsome man as the driver. It was a nice car too. She wondered why it always slowed down in front of Joe's house. She would ask Joe sometime. He would know.

CHAPTER FOUR

SAM ROMA was rather proud of himself. He lay on his side facing Cynthia Cavallo, daughter of the quarry's owner. She looked cool and beautiful in a white bathing suit, her body tall, slim, brown and flawless. Her blonde hair and blue eyes had been inherited from her Nordic mother.

It was well known that eventually Cynthia and Sam would mary. Not bad for a guy who had been brought up in one of the shacks on the Quarry Road. When his mother and father had died within a year of each other, young Sam had been sent to an orphan's home. Here, he had received more education than any of the quarry people. He had studied every text on quarry work that he could get hold of. He learned all the techniques of modern mining. The knowledge had given him a big build-up when he left the orphanage and returned to Quarry Road.

When he met Cynthia Cavallo, he had been just one of the quarry diggers. A word from Cynthia to her father—and Sam Roma was made foreman. Someday, he would be owner of the Cavallo business. But he had to play it right. He had to handle this beautiful bronzed ice-box with kid gloves. It was tough. Many were the times his blood pounded and his body was left sick and trembling from wanting her.

Even now, in the cooling evening, he was perspiring. He wanted her—now. But he had to resign himself to the fact there'd be plenty of time after marriage.

The club swimming pool slowly became deserted. It had been built recently, a community enterprise run by membership dues. Sam's one hundred dollar initiation fee had been paid by Cynthia as a birthday gift.

Cynthia pulled a terrycloth jacket around her shoulders. "It's gotten rather chilly. So hot today, too. Sam, you were nice to let those men go home today."

"Good policy—that's all. Wouldn't be good business to have any man get sick with the heat. And it sure was hot down in that hole today."

"It certainly was hot," she corrected.

"Okay, teacher. It certainly was hot." He grinned the way she liked him to.

"And must you say 'okay'?"

Sam had to force the grin to hide annoyance. "That's from force of habit, I guess. From talking to the men all day."

"Well, I think we should go now, Sam."

"Wait a while longer, dear," Sam pleaded. "It's getting dark and the crowd is thinning out. I want to kiss you so much."

"Poor darling." Her beautiful face leaned over Sam's and kissed him gently on his lips. It actually felt cool to Sam. "There," she said. "Now we must go." She got up in a single graceful movement. Sam looked longingly at her cool perfect body, then got up and followed her to the club house.

Mrs. Giambra closed the store shutters. She carefully emptied the cash register, counted the money, then dumped it all into a can. She placed the can high up on a shelf, then spread other cans in front of it. She would close up early tonight, she thought, and try to collect some money from that no good scoundrel of a Mr. Malancuni.

She thumbed through the copybook and finally located the name of Jake Malancuni. "What a scoundrel! I must go to collect the money he owes me." A quiver ran through the ample body of Mrs. Giambra. The last time she had gone, the beast had ravished her. And the time before that, he had done the same thing. She had forgotten how many times he had raped her. It happened every time that she went to collect her money. It would not happen this time, however. She would see to that. "He's just like an animal." She shivered again.

Snapping off the store lights, she went into the kitchen. She found a bag and slipped a bottle of wine into it. Then she stepped out into the darkness and locked the door behind her.

The night air was hot and mucky, hotter than in the store. As she made her way toward the quarry, she passed the people of the road, all out on their tiny porches. The Colellas were sitting out. Giovanni Colella, his scrawny chest bare, was sipping at a bottle of beer.

"Hey, Mrs. Giambra," shouted Mrs. Colella, "do you go to collect from *Il Capirosso?*"

Mrs. Giambra winced. "Yes," she answered. "I cannot stay long in business if I do not collect something."

"Ha ha," laughed Giovanni Colella. "Why do you not come to collect our bill when my wife is not home? I will pay you good. Ha ha." His loud hearty laughter resounded in the darkness.

"Be quiet, you pig," Mrs. Colella yelled at her husband. Then: "I hope you will do better this time, Mrs. Giambra." She and her husband laughed knowingly.

Mrs. Giambra muttered, "An honest woman cannot even go to collect her bills in peace." She made her way silently up the road, fearful of attracting the attention of the other tenants sitting out. Tiny beads of perspiration formed on the hairs of her upper lip. She wiped her face daintily with her handkerchief. Down at the end of the road, all was dark. She was glad of that. Soon she passed the last of the houses. Another hundred feet and the shack loomed up, dark and ugly.

"*Buona sera,* Mrs. Giambra. What can I do for you this fine evening?" The redhead's voice startled her in the darkness. She saw him then, sprawled out in front of his shack on his old army cot.

"*Buona sera,* Mr. Malancuni. I did not see you in the darkness." Mrs. Giambra shivered in spite of the heat. "Mr. Malancuni," she began her speech, "your account is past due. I cannot keep my business long, if I do not collect my money."

"Yes, I know, Mrs. Giambra." The redhead fairly exuded charm. "I wish with all my heart that I could pay you this money right now, so that you would not need to make these useless trips here. You know that I mean to pay you."

"Can't you give me anything at all?" protested Mrs. Giambra.

"Cara *mia.* If I could, you know that I would. But the company has not paid me in weeks. And I can just about make ends meet."

"You do not lie to me, do you?"

"I would not lie to you. See, tonight I am sober because I do not have anything to drink even."

"Ah, you poor man. See, I have a bottle of wine for you, if you want me to add it to your bill."

"*Cara mia.* You are so thoughtful. Here, sit down and I will share my wine with you." He moved one leg so that it dangled over the edge of the cot and made room for her.

Mrs. Giambra sat down daintily, making certain not to touch any part of his body. "I cannot stay long. I did not come on a social call, you know," she added firmly.

"Of course, I understand. But you must have one drink with me."

"Only one sip then."

The redhead began to fumble with the bottle. He got up and went into the shack. A dim light fit up for a moment, and Mrs.

Giambra looked toward the row of houses anxiously. She felt relieved when the light went out again. The redhead came out and sat heavily on the cot. He handed her a glass, then filled it up.

"You will try to have some money for me next time, then." Mrs. Giambra was trying hard to keep the visit business-like in spite of the trembling of her body at his closeness.

"But of course. Here now, drink up." Mrs. Giambra took a tiny sip. "Ah, take a good drink." The redhead patted her arm. She trembled violently, almost spilling the wine. She took a long drink and felt the warmth creep through her body and settle in her thighs.

The redhead lifted the bottle to his lips. He drank heartily with a loud gargling sound. The darkish liquid dripped down the corner of his mouth. He brought the bottle away from his lips with a loud contented smack. Then he wiped his mouth with the back of his hand. He looked at the woman's glass. It was almost empty. He poured more wine until she made a motion for him to stop.

"I cannot drink more.... I must go."

"Just finish what is in your glass. Please."

She finished the wine at one gulp. The redhead watched her with a grin. When he put the bottle to his lips again, he finished the contents.

"I must go now," said Mrs. Giambra. She started to get up. "Please let me go." her voice was a wail. She was lost. It was about to happen again. She made a feeble effort to get up, but her legs and body refused to move.

Redhead threw the empty bottle into the darkness. His hands on her shoulders were like gnarled vines holding her, drawing her to him.

Wine numbed her brain, caused her body to tingle all over. She sagged against him, breathed in the foul stink of his unwashed body.

She moaned. "Let me go." He pulled her down so that she was lying on the cot, and he was kneeling beside her on the ground. His hands moulded her ample breasts through the cotton dress, his lips in her hair.

"*Cara—Cara*" he groaned.

She opened her eyes. His red hair glistened in the moonlight. She shuddered as his face bent over hers and kissed her hard. "How ugly he is. All is lost. All is lost." Suddenly, in a frenzy: "Hurry! Hurry!"

It was over very quickly. A savage, frenzied meeting of bodies. "Ah! Ah!" she groaned and almost died. The redhead got up from her and stumbled into the shack.

The woman lay on the cot. The pale moon looked down upon her exposed thighs, glistening with perspiration. Slowly she got up. The hem of her dress dropped and covered her nakedness.

"You will pay me something next time, then, Mr. Malancuni?" she called softly into the darkness of the shack. There was no answer. She turned from the shack and made her way on uncertain legs back up the road to the store.

CHAPTER FIVE

TERESA whirled in her new dress, billowing it high above her knees. Her high proud breasts bobbled ever so slightly. She came to a stand-still and faced Joe, her arms spread out in a beckoning gesture. Her face glowed with joy. Joe grabbed her about the middle and raised her off her feet. She kissed him joyfully on the mouth.

"You look like a million bucks, Baby," he said.

"Do you really think so?"

"You bet. You know what I'd like to do right now?" A twinkle flashed in his eyes that Teresa knew very well.

"Oh, please, Joe. Do not let me take off this beautiful dress now." She pouted.

He laughed out loud. "I'm only kidding, Baby." He crushed her hard against him and was rewarded with a long warm kiss. He almost changed his mind.

She finally drew away. "Please put me down now, Joe. You are wrinkling my dress."

"I don't know now, Baby. I was only kidding before—but now I don't know."

"Please, Joe. Don't let me. I will make it up to you tonight." Her body was hot against him. He put her down reluctantly.

"Okay, Baby. Tonight then. Everybody is already at Giovanni's house anyway." And that was quite evident from the din from next door: laughter and cries of the children, loud raucous conversations of the grown-ups. It all came through, loud and clear.

"Do you think they will like me, Joe?" Teresa asked.

"I don't see how they can help it. If they don't, I'll punch them right in the nose."

"Oh, Joe, you must not do that," she answered seriously.

They were finally ready and they went out into the early twilight. Next door, at the Colella house, the party was in full swing. Sounds of music and dancing, mixed with loud talk and laughter, came clearer. A group of men sat about on the porch, drinking Angelo's best home-made wine. All the other houses on the road were dark because everyone was here at Giovanni's.

Teresa tugged at Joe's arm. "I am nervous," she whispered.

"Don't be, Baby," soothed Joe. "These people are my friends and they respect me. And they will respect you too." As they entered Giovanni's yard there was a loud roar of greetings and approval. Reaching the porch, they were instantly surrounded by the men. Teresa smiled shyly. Joe, grinning proudly, introduced her around. The names were lost on Teresa as she nodded her head to each one.

Giovanni emerged from the house with two glasses. "Hello, Joe—hello, Teresa," he yelled exuberantly. "Here, fill up the glasses for my good friend Joe and his little lady."

One of the men poured crystal-clear red wine into the glasses. "God bless you, Angelo. For you have made this wine perfect for the christening of my little one," laughed Giovanni.

"It is the best I have ever made," agreed Angelo.

Joe raised his glass. "To the new bambino, my good friend. And may you be blessed with many many more." There was a loud cry of assent and everyone drank to the toast. Teresa sipped hers and liked it. A long time ago, she had once tasted wine.

Giovanni faced her. "You know. All the ladies are supposed to kiss the happy father. What's the matter, Joe?" he turned to Joe. "Didn't you explain this to her?"

Joe grinned. "No, I forgot. That's right, Teresa. You have to kiss him. All the men nodded, grinning. Teresa pecked lightly as Giovanni puckered up his lips expectantly.

At this moment, Maria Colella came out on the porch. Joe grabbed her and gave her a resounding kiss.

"Hey, Joe," yelled Giovanni, "you must not do that. That is all you have to do to my Maria and she becomes pregnant."

Maria, getting into the spirit of the fun, laughed heartily. "Yes, with you maybe, Giovanni, I become pregnant with a kiss. But with this one—" she poked Joe in the ribs—"it would be impossible."

"Some day, I'll show you, Maria," laughed Joe.

"It would be okay with me, Joe," kidded Giovanni. "I will trade with you anytime." He grinned, then let out a yell, twisting aside as his wife grabbed at him.

"Hey, let's see the baby," said Joe.

With his arm about the glowing Maria, Joe led the way into the house. Giovanni followed with Teresa. He wanted to put his arm around her but decided not to. Later when he was a little drunk, he would put his arms about her and he would dance with her.

Inside the house, two short swarthy musicians were playing. One fingered an old time-beaten guitar, its veneer peeling. The other man played an old-country accordion, small and battered but letting forth with a lusty bellow. The music was off-key but melodic. They were playing a saltarella, an old-country jig of sorts. The children too were dancing and stamping their feet.

Around the walls at every available nook sat the women. Mrs. Giambra, the store-keeper, held the new-born baby. Her dark skin turned even darker when she saw Joe. She held out the baby to Maria. It made tiny animal noises and it's tiny wrinkled head sagged to one side. It's eyes stared aimlessly about, seeing nothing.

Giovanni stuck out his chest. "Please meet Dominic, after my grandfather."

"Hello, Dominic," said Joe. He took a five dollar bill from out of his pocket, and, borrowing a pin from Maria, pinned it on the infant's dress.

"Oh, how beautiful he is," said Teresa. She kissed it gently on the cheek.

"God bless you," murmured Maria under her breath. This to prevent *mal-occhi* or over-looks. As every-one knew, a child or a grown-up for that matter would surely become ill if a compliment wasn't supplemented with a "God bless you," to ward off the evil.

"Can I hold him?" asked Teresa. Maria handed the baby to Teresa and she cradled it in her arms.

"She is beautiful," said Giovanni aside to Joe. "She needs a little one." He winked. Joe grinned. The baby began to cry and Teresa handed it back to Maria after kissing it tenderly.

In a little while, the children gave up the living room floor to the adults who had come indoors for some earnest dancing. The wine flowed freely. Angelo had made two trips to his house for more wine. The women danced with energy and took it seriously. The men, mostly drunk by now, danced gingerly, as though afraid to trust their legs.

The Renaldo brothers played the same songs over and over. When their limited repertoire was exhausted, they started all over again. They had been playing *La Tarantella* for the past fifteen minutes and most of the couples were exhausted.

Only Teresa and Giovanni remained on the floor. They whirled, twirled and stamped their feet to the beat of hand-clapping. The musicians played with energy, refusing to quit until the last of the dancers had given up. They played faster and faster as the onlookers shouted their encouragement and approval. And soon it was obvious that Giovanni was tiring.

"Joe! Joe!" called the crowd. Without a change in tempo, Joe took Giovanni's place. Giovanni slumped into a chair someone vacated for him. Joe, however, could not keep up the furious pace for long.

Mrs. Giambra sat in a corner, a half-filled glass of wine in her hand. She stared at the dancing couple with a glazed look of fascinated dislike. It showed in the tight lines of her mouth and in the tenseness of her body. As she stared at the vivacious beauty of Teresa she realized with a sinking heart that Joe was lost to her. Her store could not compete with the girl's youth and vitality. Mrs. Giambra wondered why the redhead had not come to the party. She could have asked him to pay up on some of his bill.

She finished her glass of wine. As a matter of fact, she would go to his shack and demand it right now. She got up on wobbily legs. Teresa and Joe had to stop dancing to keep from knocking her down. She walked gingerly, staring straight ahead.

"Hey, Mrs. Giambra, where are you going?" asked Giovanni.

Mrs. Giambra didn't answer. Out of the house she went, and up the road toward the redhead's shack. She walked like a sleepwalker, her body rigid. She stumbled and almost fell. Soon she was lost in the darkness.

Giovanni laughed so hard he almost fell out of his chair. Teresa looked at him, puzzled. Everyone else began to laugh. Joe explained.

"She is going to collect her bill from the redhead."

"At this hour?" asked Teresa innocently. This sent every one into hysterics. Teresa finally joined them, though not quite sure why. She laughed heartily when Giovanni toppled off the chair and sprawled on the floor.

A while later the men and women gathered in the center of the room. Most of the men had glasses of wine. Giovanni held a bottle. He poured whenever he could get someone to hold his glass still. And they sang an old wine-drinking song.

Soon they were singing the songs they had brought from their beautiful Italian cities, from the vineyards and from the farms. The songs of their youth. Songs that brought back memories of their native villages and towns. Of the harvest, love, sorrow, death. They sang of these. And for a short poignant time, they were back at the places of their birth.

A youngster rushed into the house. "The cops! The cops!"

Two policemen appeared on the porch and looked in through the screen door.

Giovanni opened the door wide. "Come in, my friends," he invited. They grinned broadly as they came in. "Hey! Wine for the policemen!" Giovanni yelled.

Joe brought two glasses and a bottle. One of the policemen recognized Joe and nodded. They took the glasses, protestingly but grinning. The glasses were filled.

"Drink hearty," said Giovanni. "It is for the christening of my new son, Dominic."

"Salute," said the policeman who recognized Joe. They raised the glasses.

"*Prosido*," said Giovanni.

The officers finished the wine with little effort. Joe started to fill the glasses again, but the policemen covered them with their palms.

"We're not supposed to be drinking. Thanks," said the same one. They waved to everyone, turned and left the house. Joe walked with them to their prowl car. "Don't let the party get out of hand, Joe." They got into the car.

"No. Don't worry, Kelly. They're good folks. They'll be in bed before another hour is up."

"Okay, then. So long. Oh, by the way, Joe. That was pretty good wine."

"The best," said Joe.

"My wife's old man makes some. But it don't compare with that stuff you got in there."

"Yeah, it's pretty good stuff," agreed the other officer, speaking for the first time.

"Wait here a minute," said Joe. He went into the house. The policemen grinned at each another. Joe returned in a few minutes with a bottle of wine.

"Make sure the sergeant gets a drink."

Kelly grinned. "Tell the folks thanks, eh, Joe."

"You bet."

"So long."

"So long." The car drove off.

It was eleven-thirty when the party broke up. Joe and Teresa were the last to leave. Teresa promised to come early next morning to help Maria Colella clean up. All along the road, the houses lit up. They stayed lit for fifteen or twenty minutes, then went out. The road once more was quiet and still.

Joe and Teresa undressed. Joe had gotten drunk, as had every other male in the community. At the moment, he wished only to lay down and go to sleep. Teresa, on the other hand, felt light-headed and gay. Her stomach was warm from the wine. She had not drunk too much, and the blood in her veins was still coursing wildly from the dancing. As she looked at the huge bulging muscles of Joe's body on the bed, her throat felt tight and her heart pounded. Her legs suddenly felt weak. She remembered that there was something she had promised Joe. But he was asleep. Poor Joe. She would let him sleep.

Down to her slip only, she turned off the light, went to the window and raised the shade. A wave of cool air singed into the room. A beam of moonlight shone across the bed, rippling across Joe's muscled body. Teresa lay down beside Joe. She kissed his cheek, then moved as far as was possible away from him. Her intentions were good.

A half hour passed. She tried with all her might to fall asleep. But her blood was still coursing to the tune of *La Tarantella*. Sleep would not come. Slowly, she raised herself on one elbow. She leaned over Joe. Her lips found his mouth. They lingered gently there. Then she kissed his throat and chest. Her hand was insistently caressing. Joe stirred. Slowly, in spite of his deep sleep he began to respond. In a sleepy, drunken daze he reached for the woman at his side. She locked her mouth on his and gratefully went into his arms.

CHAPTER SIX

T HE next morning Joe Carato felt very tired. He looked at Teresa as she went about her household duties and he felt a dull emptiness in his loins. It was almost a month now since she had come to stay. And until now he had had such a consuming need for her that he had seldom gone out. Except for the hours at work, and the time for eating and sleeping, all of his time had been spent in making love to Teresa. He simply could not get enough of her. And she, although not encouraging (except for last night) or discouraging him, was always ready. In her simple mind, it was the least she could do to repay Joe for his kindness.

"I must be getting old," muttered Joe to himself. "And me only forty-two. This girl will sure as hell be my death."

Suddenly he wanted someone to talk to. Someone who would say something besides "yes," or "no," as Teresa did. He had found out very quickly that her conversation was acutely limited. He had noted the painful expression in her eyes when she had to answer a question about her past. If she could do it with a "yes" or "no," she would do so. But when she had to explain something, she was completely lost. Therefore, when Joe saw the pained look come into her eyes, he would mercifully change the subject. For this, she was grateful.

Joe was now tired of this. He wanted to hear someone talk. He wanted to hear men cursing and telling dirty jokes. He wanted to hear some good-natured swearing. He wanted to swear with them and swap jokes with them.

"Listen, Teresa baby. I'm going out to see what the men are doing." His voice was apologetic, as though he were expecting an argument. He wasn't sure of her reactions. He had never had occasion to leave before.

"Yes, Joe. You go out. Go have a few drinks with the men. It is not good for you to be in all the time." She came and kissed him softly on the mouth.

Joe thought: How lucky can a guy be? He felt a tenderness well up for this girl. He grabbed her for a moment and kissed her. He would see what Giovanni, next door, was doing. He went out on the tiny porch, yelled.

"Hey, Giovanni!"

Giovanni came out immediately. He wore only his pants. He was even barefooted. "What's the matter, Joe?" It was the first time Joe had called for him since the girl had come.

"Nothing's the matter," laughed Joe. "I just wanted to have a couple of drinks with somebody."

"Like the old times, eh, Joe?"

"Yeah, like old times."

"Wait, I go to put on my shirt. We will go to see the redhead. Maybe Angelo is there and we will play some cards." Giovanni disappeared into the house. Joe went in to speak to Teresa. He really felt bad about leaving her. He felt so certain that she was hurt.

"Teresa," he began softly," I am going with Giovanni to play cards. I'll be back early."

"Yes, you go, Joe."

"You sure you'll be all right?"

"I will be fine. There are some things of yours that I want to sew. You go."

Joe looked at the girl wonderingly. Then, impulsively, he grabbed her and kissed her soundly. It was only meant to be a good-natured kiss. Her soft, feminine body touched and pressed against him for only a split second. He laughed out loud. I am not getting old, after all, he thought. Only moments before, he had felt old and beaten. If he stayed a moment longer, Giovanni would have to go to the redhead's by himself. He strode outside, afraid to trust himself. Afraid that his body would disregard the orders of his mind. He found Giovanni ready. They made their way toward the quarry and the redhead's shack.

"Well, I'll be a sonofabitch!" roared redheaded Jake when he saw the two approaching. "Look, Angelo, Joe is free again." Angelo was the oldest of the four. He spoke little English, having been too old to learn the new language. With him, however, he had brought the secret of the wine-makers of the tiny village he had left behind. And for years his friends on the Road had enjoyed the fruits of his knowledge. *"Ha bella Madonna"* he said. *"Guarda, e' vivo."*

"Sure, he's alive," responded the redhead. "But he must be half dead from that woman of his. Eh, Joe?"

"It's a good way to die," laughed Joe.

"You don't have to die from it, Joe," said the redhead. "Like I said, let me get a piece once in a while. We can both enjoy it, and live, too."

"You too ugly," chided Angelo.

"Yes," agreed Giovanni. "What would a girl like that want with one so ugly as you, *Capirosso?*"

"You know I'm only kidding, Joe," said the redhead. "I just talk to have fun. But you better watch that snaky Sam Roma. He's got his eyes open for that woman of yours."

There was a strained silence. They all looked at Joe to see his reactions. Beads of perspiration formed on his forehead. He looked at once hurt and shocked. Redhead realized instantly that he had said something wrong.

"What do you mean, Redhead?" asked Joe at last. "Has that no-good bastard been going around my house while I work?"

Redhead did not answer. He realized he had started something but didn't know how to explain himself.

"What about it, Giovanni?" asked Joe. "Maria should know. Has he been nosing around?"

"Do not listen to the redheaded fool," answered Giovanni.

"*Non li sentire,*" agreed Angelo. "Do not listen to him."

But Joe was not to be put off so easily. He leaned over the sprawled out redhead. "If you don't explain yourself, I will break that ugly body of yours in half."

"I'm not a fool, Joe," said the redhead defiantly. "I see what goes on around here. I see that sonofabitchin' bastard slow down every time he passes your house."

Joe looked at Giovanni. He knew that his next-door neighbor would not lie to him.

Giovanni nodded his head. "But what does that prove? He is curious. Everyone from the quarry is curious about your woman. Sam is curious too. He wishes to see what she looks like. If she is fat or if she is skinny. But I am sure that he has not seen her. No one has seen her since the party. So do not listen to this redheaded idiot."

"Okay," said the redhead, maybe I am crazy. And maybe you're right." He was relieved that the tension had been broken. But inwardly he was excited about the seeds of doubt he had sown. "But I would watch him," he concluded.

"It is enough of this foolish talk," said Giovanni. "Let us get along with the game."

"Yeah," agreed Joe. "Let's forget Sam Roma. I'll take care of him when the time comes. Where's the cards, Redhead?"

The redhead grunted as he got off the cot. He went inside. Giovanni and Angelo looked apprehensively at Joe. He was not one to bear a grudge, they knew. But a man's woman was not something to take lightly in the community. They had been truly worried. Now, they breathed a little easier. The redhead reappeared and threw a worn out pack of cards onto the cot. He sat down on an end of it. The others found wooden crates.

"What will we play?" asked Giovanni. He mixed the cards thoroughly.

"*Facciamo una partita di scopa,*" said Angelo.

"Yeah, let's play some sweep," agreed Joe. "I guess we'll play as we are." He was seated opposite the redhead, making them partners. Giovanni put the deck down on the cot. Joe cut, Giovanni dealt.

CHAPTER SEVEN

SAM ROMA'S temperature rose to fever pitch at the closeness of Cynthia Cavallo. It always did when they danced. They were dancing slightly apart because of the sweltering heat. But the brush of her breast or the pressure of her thighs against his body was enough to raise his temperature many degrees. He wanted to crush her to him, to feel her body full against him. But the damned heat was just too much. And what the hell were they doing here, dancing, anyway?

"Come on, sweetheart, let's get out of here," he whispered. "It's too darn hot to be dancing."

"Oh, darling. It's not so terribly hot. If you wouldn't hold me so close, I'm sure you would be comfortable"

"Please, Cynthia, let's sit by the pool at least. I'm suffocating with this jacket on and everything." Sam could feel the sweat rolling down his back.

"I wish you would explain yourself better, Sam. Now what on earth do you mean by *everything?*"

Sam had an urge to pound his bony fist into her cool, beautiful face. "I mean this dancing in such heat is crazy. We are the only ones on the floor." His voice was harsh and the words clipped. The girl smiled up at him.

"Oh, darling, I've made you angry with me."

"No you haven't, Cynthia. It's this damned heat."

The girl looked at the handsomely sullen face. She knew that she was the envy of all the girls of her crowd. Sam had an animal magnetism that attracted a woman at first glance. He had the build of a fighter and the handsome face of a movie idol. And his eyes could catch a woman's eyes and hold them until she could feel her heart pound and her knees tremble.

It had happened to her when she had first seen Sam Roma. But the cool Norse temperment inherited from her mother had been enough to overcome her first physical attraction. It had been difficult, and Sam had almost made her yield physically on their third date. The incident had left her weak and trembling with a terrific headache. But after that, it had been easier and easier to repel him. He was now, like a little lamb, satisfied with whatever crumb of affection she would throw to him. She had become the stronger of the two.

Not that she did not feel the physical attraction for him any longer. She did, in fact. But only in the safety of her room did she allow her feelings to overcome her. Here, she allowed her mind to be fogged by his caresses. In a dreamy state, she would allow his hands to caress her naked body. She would feel his lips wander over her, and her body would respond ecstatically, even to the final fulfillment. She had spent many an idle hour in such rapturous fantasies.

From what she had heard and read about the sex act she knew it would be an exquisite feeling, although it had never really been satisfactorily explained how one would feel. Still, she felt a thrill just from the thought of the act. There were times when she wished she had allowed Sam to have her. Mostly, though, she was glad she hadn't. She felt she would marry Sam, someday. Right now, however, she was content to have him dangling at her fingertips, and to watch other women drool over him. She would hold him off as long as it was possible. For the longer she waited for the wedding night, the more poignant would be the thrill of fulfillment.

Cynthia was wise, as women mostly are. And when she saw the anger in Sam's face, she knew she must not push him too far. There were too many eager females around. She smiled sweetly at Sam. "All right, darling. Let's go sit by the pool if you want."

Later, in her convertible, they parked by the side of a lake. The parking lights of several other cars could be seen here and there. A slight breeze had begun to rustle the leaves on an overhanging limb. For the first time in several days, Sam felt cool. He had removed his jacket, and goose-pimples formed where the breeze blew across his damp shirt.

Tonight, he felt an inner excitement. As though something was about to happen. A tiny flame was smouldering within him. He felt it growing, kindled by the nearness, yet distant reserve of this girl. Something had to give. If only she would let herself go for once. He had known many girls. Almost without exception, they had been easy conquests. They had given themselves easily, eagerly. They had been quick affairs and hadn't lasted long.

Cynthia was as hard to get as they had been easy. Sam's ego suffered no end with the knowledge that here was a woman, desirable, beautiful and wholly unattainable. Lord, how he would like to smash that cool, beautiful face. His hands trembled as he lighted a cigarette. He took two puffs, then flipped it toward the lake.

The girl stirred. Her arm crept around his and tightened so that he could feel her breast hard against his forearm. Her leg pressed heavily against him. She leaned her head on his shoulder. "It's so beautiful out here," she sighed.

"Cynthia, honey, when can we get married?"

"Soon."

"I can't stand this much longer."

"What's that dear?" she asked, dreamily.

"You know. This waiting." He half expected her to tell him to explain himself.

"I know it's hard, dear. Please be patient It's just as hard for me."

"You seem to be enjoying it," he said bitterly.

"Sam, that's not fair."

"I know it's not fair—to me."

She turned and kissed him lightly on the mouth. "Please be sweet. Don't spoil such a beautiful evening by arguing."

"I can't help it. I want you so bad, it's driving me crazy."

"Please be patient," she appealed. "It would only spoil everything."

"Then let's get married right away," he blurted out.

"Oh, Sam," she said impatiently. "You know how impossible that would be. Mother would want a big wedding. And a big wedding takes time."

"Is it so necessary to you to have a big wedding? When two people are in love, just a two-dollar license is enough. Plenty of people don't even worry about getting married."

"I'm not one of those other people, Sam. Don't ever forget *that*, Sam." Her voice had an edge, and it sent a chill up his spine. She started to loosen her hold on his arm. He half turned and wrapped his arms about her and kissed her cruelly, deliberately trying to hurt her. For an instant she responded. But when his hand went to her breast, she stiffened. Before he realized what had happened she had torn from his arms. "Perhaps you would like to rape me," she said coldly.

"I wish I had the nerve," he whispered hoarsely. "Maybe that would make a woman out of you." He sat back in the seat.

She looked at him, shocked and surprised. He had never talked like this before. Without a word, she started the car and drove carefully down the dirt road to the highway, making sure to avoid the deep ruts and bumps. Once on the highway she headed for the club with a great burst of speed.

Later, Sam Roma drove his car hard toward the quarry. It had become a habit with him to drive out toward the quarry. Even when things went well with Cynthia and himself, he would find himself driving out toward the tiny community. He knew why, too. Always in his mind, lurked the faint hope that he would get a glimpse of Joe's woman. He had yet to see her. The curiosity was beginning to get the best of him.

Now, as he drove toward the quarry, he thought of Cynthia. That bitch. That teasing bitch! He should have raped her. That's what she needed. If only he had the nerve. He wouldn't be able to figure her out in a million years. What the hell was she made of anyway?

The redhead had been right, as much as Sam hated to admit it. "She ain't for you," the redhead had told him once. "She's class. And you ain't nothing." Sam had almost punched the old man for saying it. But Jake had been right. "Why don't you wise up and marry one of your own kind," he had said, "Now you take Joe. He's got the kind of woman that's good for you. A good-looking babe, too. And all she wants out of a guy is a roof over her head. Don't go getting ideas, though. Cause Joe would kick the living spit out of you." He had laughed hard as Sam stomped away.

Usually when Sam came down to Quarry Road, it was rather late. He seldom left Cynthia before midnight. The community here was almost always asleep. As he drew near he slowed down, mildly startled to see lights on in all the houses. Only then did he realize the time was only nine-thirty. Cynthia had left him off at the club and had gone home. She had been very angry.

Joe's house was lit up, but no one was in sight. Down at the end of the street, he could see the light on at the redhead's shack. Still smarting under the memory of the redhead's taunting remarks, he jammed his foot on the gas pedal. The car roared up the road. He would show that ugly old man. He'd teach him to mind his own business.

The four men had tired of playing cards and were playing morra, a game played by tossing out the fingers of one hand, then calling out a number up to ten. The one who called the correct sum of both players won.

"*Cinque,*" shouted Giovanni, as he threw two fingers.

"*Quatro,*" yelled Joe, throwing in three. "Ah, you win again with your five. Some day, I will beat you a game." He laughed good-naturedly.

Giovanni turned to Angelo. "Your turn now. I will beat you and be champion.

"*Cinque!*" Angelo yelled, putting out three fingers.

"*Nove!*" shouted Giovanni as he put out five fingers. Neither won. They threw again.

"*Cinque,*" called Giovanni with one finger.

"*Sette,*" said Angelo and threw four. Too late, he tried to change the amount of fingers. Giovanni had won again.

"You're too damn lucky," said the redhead. "You always win."

"Not lucky, *Capirosso.* My father taught me to play this game when I was a little boy. No one could beat my father at it. And he always said that to win you must read the mind of your opponent. You must know how many fingers they will throw."

Joe guffawed, "Okay. So now, see if you can read my mind. What am I thinking of?"

Giovanni looked wise. He counted each one of the men with exaggerated motions. Then he put the tips of his fingers to his temples. "I see four glasses of Angelo's best wine. That is what you are thinking of, my friend."

"You're right again, Giovanni. Don't get up, Redhead. I'll get it." Joe got up from the crate and went into the shack. In a moment he was out again with a bottle and four glasses. He handed out the glasses, then poured out the wine. It looked darkish in the dim light. They drank slowly.

"It has gotten too hot," ventured Giovanni.

Jake nodded. "It's this damned heat. Can't keep anything cool. My piece of ice melted long ago."

From the other end of the road two headlights came hurtling toward them. The roar of the motor lashed the peaceful night. The quarry people wondered sleepily what was happening.

"Now who the hell can that be?" asked Joe. Deep down, he knew.

As though answering Joe's question, Redhead ventured an opinion. "From the way he's driving like he owns the road, I'd say it was that sonofabitchin' Sam Roma."

Before the car came to a screeching halt with the headlights full on the group, they knew that Redhead was right. Sam Roma came storming out of the car. "What the hell is this supposed to be?" he shouted. He went over to the redhead and towered over him. The redhead remained in his sprawled-out position. Sam's shadow, formed by the headlights of the car, absorbed the whole group. For a moment, everyone stared in bewildered silence. Finally, Joe spoke up.

"We ain't doing anything, Sam. Just drinking some wine and keeping the redhead company."

"You stay out of this," growled Sam. He tinned to Jake. "This is company property, and you're supposed to be watching it. That's what you get paid for."

"We are all watching it," quipped Giovanni.

"Shut up, Giovanni. You guys are all smart, making with the wise-cracks. How about it, Redhead? What have you got to say about it?"

"I dont have a damned thing to say to you, Sam. Why don't you get the hell out of here and leave us alone? Ain't nothing going to happen to the company property."

"You better watch the way you talk to me. You hear? I'm going to see that the boss hears about this."

"Kiss my foot," snorted the redhead.

With a growl, Sam grabbed the old man by his shirt front and half lifted him out of the cot.

The redhead spat full in Sam's face.

"Why you—" Sam screamed. He raised his fist to punch the obnoxiously grinning face. At this moment, Joe grabbed the upraised arm by the wrist and twisted. Sam tried to wrench his arm free, but Joe's fingers were like steel bands. Sam found it impossible to even move his arm. With one turning, pivoting motion, Sam let loose the redhead's shirt and swung at Joe's groin. Joe doubled up with a grunt, and Sam drove his freed right fist into the side of Joe's face. Joe went sprawling.

From his sitting position, Joe looked foolishly at the men. The pain started to gather in his groin. He saw Sam start for his car. And suddenly it was quiet. So awfully quiet. It was broken by Joe's scream of agony mingled with fury as he raised himself off the ground. He reached Sam as he was entering his car.

Attracted by the commotion, the entire populace of the tiny community ran toward the shack.

Joe outweighed Sam by some fifty pounds. And as if this were not enough, Joe had the experience of some thirty fights in the ring. Joe's first vicious blow to Sam's head left him helpless. The car alone held Sam up. With a savagery that had accumulated and fermented in his system through all the years of working under Sam Roma, Joe drove his ham-like fists at the unguarded body before him. He struck wildly, his punches landing at random on soggy, quivering flesh. As though from far far away he could hear the screams of the women, as Sam turned into a gory, bloody mess before their eyes. The men looked on in stunned silence, unable to move, fascinated by the sight before them.

Out of the crowd ran Teresa. "Joe! Stop, Joe!" she screamed.

CHAPTER EIGHT

HER voice penetrated through the hate fog to Joe's senses, and he held his blows. Sam's inert body slumped to the ground. Joe backed away from the body, only now realizing what he had done. Sam Roma looked so still.

Teresa knelt besides him, wiped some of the blood from his face with the hem of her dress. The sight of this man, half dead and helpless, had given her a strength she had never realized she possessed. It was strange to her, and it frightened her. This man, whom she had seen only from afar as he drove by, had caused it. Or had he? She was confused. Would she have wiped the bloody face of someone else?

"You almost killed this man, Joe," she said simply. "You almost killed him."

Joe's head was cleared by now. "I didn't mean it, Baby," he said. "I didn't know what I was doing. Honest! I didn't know what I was doing." The crowd had begun to mill about, closer, trying to get a good view of the prostrated Sam. Joe turned to them. "You saw what happened. He tried to beat up on the redhead. Then he socked me when I tried to stop him. I didn't start it. Ask the redhead. Ask Giovanni."

"You had better take him to a hospital, Joe. If you don't, he will die. He is hurt bad, Joe. Very bad." Teresa did not turn, and her voice went on in a sing-song fashion.

"Yeah, Baby. I think you're right. I'll take him right down to the hospital." Joe had knelt down at her side and had taken a close look at his handiwork. Sam Roma was in serious condition. There was no doubt about that. Giovanni had come closer, and he cocked his head so that he could distinguish Sam Roma's distorted features.

"I will help you, Joe," he said soberly.

With the help of some of the other men, they got Sam into the front seat of the sedan. Giovanni got into the back and held Sam upright, at the same time holding a piece of cloth to his bleeding cuts. Joe got into the driver's seat, and they drove off.

In the dim light of the shack, Teresa made a tiny though resolute figure. Her hand still clutching the blood-stained hem of her dress, she held it at arm's length, leaving her legs bare well above her knees. The low whispering could be heard all about as the crowd started to break up into groups. There were sly glances from everyone, the men's stares inadvertently slipping down to her bare legs.

Suddenly there was a shout from the crowd near the redhead. "Somebody come and see what is wrong with *Capirosso!*"

In a moment, the crowd had gathered about the redhead. Through it all, he had remained sprawled out on the cot. His eyes were dazed, and he was gasping for breath, every wheezy breath an effort. His gnarled hands, twisted in agony, were pressing against his heart, trying to ease the pain. "The pills! The pills in the cabinet!" he managed to gasp out. Someone ran into the hut and out again. He had a small plastic jar with several pills in it, and a glass of water.

Teresa watched as they gave the redhead a pill and a drink of water. She watched the ugly red face as the pain left it. She shuddered, unable to take her eyes away from him. She heard someone mention the name, Dr. Bagnaro, and saw a small boy run down Quarry Road toward the town.

Ten minutes later a car came up the road. It stopped near the crowd. The small boy and an elderly man stepped out. The man was carrying a small, black leather satchel. After a check with his stethoscope, the doctor said:

"You can't stay here any longer. You need plenty of rest. A hospital or at least someplace where somebody can take care of you. I've warned you before, Mr. Malancuni. You can't stay here alone."

"Take him to the house of Joe Carato. I will take care of him." Everyone turned at Teresa's voice. She had not moved from the spot and still stared intently at the pock-marked face.

The redhead smiled, and his face lost some of its hideousness. "No, kind lady," he said. "I don't want to impose on you and my friend Joe. I'll be all right."

The doctor shook his head. "I insist. You must get plenty of rest, or I will not be responsible. Someone must help you."

Teresa thrilled at the unquestionable certainty in her mind. "Doctor, I am sure Joe would want it this way. Would you drive Mr. Malancuni to Joe Carato's house?"

"I would be happy to do so, good lady. You are very kind." The doctor beckoned two men from the crowd. "Please help Mr. Malancuni into my car."

They got on either side of the redhead and took him by the arms.

"No, no!" he cried. "Leave me alone." He began to struggle with the two men.

The doctor faced him. "Do you want to drop dead—here and now?" he asked sternly.

The redhead struggled no longer. He submitted to the men's aid, leaning heavily on them. They helped him into the car, opposite the driver's seat. Then they piled into the rear of the car.

"Come, my good woman," said the doctor. He touched Teresa's elbow.

"It is not far. I will walk," she said. She began walking toward the house. She heard the motor of the car start up as the doctor backed up the car slowly into the crowd. She saw the resentful look that Mrs. Giambra gave her as she walked by her. Suddenly she had a headache. It had been too much for her. Would Joe scold her for letting them take the redhead into his house? She had acted out of turn, she knew. Would he be angry? The car passed her and stopped before the house. She arrived soon after. The men were already out of the car and waiting. She went into the house and lit the lights.

"You can bring him in now." Her voice sounded muffled from inside the house. The two men once more took their places on either side of the redhead, helping him out of the car and into the house. He dragged heavily between them, uncomplaining now.

The girl directed them into the extra bedroom where she had pulled down the sheet on the bed. Redhead sat down heavily on its edge. He started to bend over to untie his shoes, but the girl stopped him. She gently but firmly pushed at his shoulders until he was flat on his back.

The two men were standing at the door grinning and sneaking an occasional look at her rear as she leaned over the redhead. She reached for his belt, and he squealed and grabbed at his pants. The men laughed out loud. Even the somber doctor, standing on the other side of the bed, let a smile escape.

"Very well, then," the girl said. She turned to the men. "Please, will you take his clothing off?" The two men would have done headsprings, at the moment, if she had asked. She left the room. They went over to the redhead and forcefully began stripping him down despite his protestations. They had to hold their breath, the stink from his body was so overpowering.

"You are a lucky dog, *Capirosso*," said one.

"Yes. I wish that I was sick like you," added the other.

"Go to hell," growled the redhead.

"Hey, Redhead," said the first man. "You must watch out for Joe. Do not get fresh with his woman."

The other man chuckled. "He is half dead. He could not do much."

"It is no difference. He would get fresh with the undertaker at his own death, if it was a she undertaker."

The doctor was smiling broadly. "He'd better not do anything. Nothing but just lay there in that bed, or he will need an undertaker."

"Ah, but what a way to die, eh, Redhead," said one, grinning.

"Go to hell," said Redhead.

By now, they were through undressing him, and he lay in the bed in his long drawers. They were a darkish gray from the accumulated dirt and perspiration of a month. The smell was almost unbearable. "Maybe the girl will give you a bath herself," said one. He held his nose in comic relief from the smell. "He does need a bath. Do you not think so, Doctor?" They heard the girl coming back.

"Cover me, you fools!" cried the redhead.

The men caught the sheet and pulled it up around his neck. Still the foul stench permeated the room. The girl had changed into a clean housecoat that hugged her body. The two men kept their eyes averted until she had passed by, then they stole lingering glances at her rear. She went to the bed and leaned over to fix the sheets. She turned away, her face twisted in nauseous disgust as the acrid smell hit her. She looked helplessly at the doctor. Then she spied the pile of clothing on the floor.

"Please, will you take these out and put them in the wash tub?" she asked one of the men. He obeyed, holding his nose and grinning.

She faced the doctor. "Will he be able to wash himself?"

"He will be able to wash himself. But I would suggest that you wait for Joe Carato to come home. Joe will help him tonight at least. He does need it, doesn't he?" The doctor smiled kindly.

"Yes, he does," she agreed. She turned to the other two. The one had just returned from taking out the clothing. "Thank you very much. I do not think that we will need you any longer." She almost touched one of them as she passed by to lead them out and he stumbled back, clumsily, trying to avoid the contact. They followed her to the front door. "Thank you again," she said. She flashed them a brilliant smile. They left reluctantly.

The doctor was just putting away his stethoscope when she got back to the bedroom. "He is a lot better now," he told her. "This one was a mild attack like the others. But the next may be the last"

"He is very sick, then, Doctor?"

The doctor nodded his head.

Teresa said, "We will see that he gets better. I am sure that Joe will be glad to help his friend."

"I am sure of it." He turned to the redhead. "Don't forget to take those pills. And you should be happy to know that you have such good friends." He followed Teresa to the door. He paused before opening it. He looked at her and his face softened into a warm smile. "You are very kind," he said. Then he left, closing the door softly behind him.

It was an hour later when Joe returned. He found her in the kitchen. She had put all of the redhead's clothing in a big metal wash-tub to soak. He grabbed her in his arms as he usually did when he came home. She stiffened at his touch. And when he kissed her at the cleft of her bosom there was no response, no shiver of excitement.

"Your friend, the redheaded one, is in the other bed," she said simply.

"What!"

"He is sick and he needs a bath. Will you please help him?"

"What the hell is he doing here? How did he get here?"

"He had a heart attack and will need help. He will need someone to take care of him." She said it simply and calmly.

Joe ran to the bedroom, and there was the ugly face of the redhead, grinning up at him. "What the hell happened to you?" he grinned back.

"It's my heart, Joe. It always was in bad shape."

"You never told me."

Redhead shrugged his shoulders. "What's the use, Joe? There's nothing you can do for me. Or anybody, for that matter.'

"You could have moved in here a long time ago. That stinking shack ain't the best place in the world for a guy in your condition."

"Then it's alright for me to stay? I was kind of worried that you might not like the idea. And that you'd give your woman hell for it."

"You know you're always welcome here, you ugly, redheaded bastard."

Teresa came to the doorway. "Your friend needs a bath very much, Joe."

As much as Joe was used to the smell of sweat, he became conscious of the acrid smell in the room. He held his breath. The room had not smelled like this since Teresa had moved in. "Okay, Baby," he said. "I'll give him a bath. It'll probably be the first one in a year."

The girl did not smile at the quip. She left the room. From the bedroom she heard the two men laughing. Joe mentioned twelve stitches and a possible broken rib, and she knew that he referred to the man he had beaten up.

She had recognized the man when she had stopped the fight, despite the bloody, battered features. It was the same handsome young man that always slowed down and looked toward the house when he rode by. And of late, she had made it a point to be at the window when he passed, though hidden behind the shade.

She felt bitter toward Joe tonight. As they laughed and recounted the events of the night, she wanted to scream, and she felt an overpowering urge to run into the room and claw the two men. She was relieved when the talk from the next room was finally drowned out by the sound of running water and the bathroom door being shut.

Later, the girl sat before the mirror, brushing her hair. She wore only a slip. Her nipples showed dark through the thin fabric.

Joe sat moodily on the bed. He had stripped down to his shorts. He glanced at the girl furtively. She hadn't said a word since he had come away from the redhead. He had never seen her like this, and he was puzzled. He did not like it at all. She ignored his presence. "What's the matter, Baby?" he ventured.

She did not answer.

There was a long moment of silence. He tried again. "I'm glad you brought the redhead here. He's a pretty sick guy."

"You are not angry with me then? I was afraid that you would not like what I did."

Joe felt relief surge through him at the sound of her voice. "No, Baby! I'm glad you did it."

The girl returned into her shell. Joe remained silent for a moment, not knowing how to make a new approach. "The old redhead sure stunk up the place," he said finally.

"Yes, he needed a bath very much," she answered solemnly.

More silence. Joe gave up. He lay down on the bed, deciding to wait her out. She would let him know what was bothering her. He never had to wait this long before, though. Finally she spoke.

"Did you hurt him bad, Joe?" She did not miss a stroke of the brush.

"No. Some stitches and maybe a broken rib."

"Why did you do it?"

"He had it coming. He caused the redhead to get the attack, you know."

"You almost killed him."

"Nah! Sam's tough. I kind of felt sorry for him afterwards. But he's had it coming. Maybe it'll teach him a lesson."

"I did not think you could be so brutal. This is the same Sam that you always complain about? Your foreman?"

"Yeah, that's Sam all right. So you know he deserves it."

"But you were so—" She hesitated, racking her brain for another word to use. She couldn't think of one. "You were so brutal. You could have killed him, if I had not stopped you."

"Aw forget it, Baby. Come on to bed."

"I will sleep on the sofa."

"Aw, Baby!"

"I am sorry, Joe. I could not stand your arms around me tonight."

Joe was thoroughly upset now. This was worse than he had thought. He got out of the bed and went to her.

"I'm really sorry, Baby." He held her by the shoulders, his huge hands hiding half of her upper arms. If she'd give in just a little he would crush her to him. But she didn't. He felt her tense. She looked as though she were about to burst out crying. His heart went out to her. He grabbed her up and put her on the bed, gently, as though lifting a small child.

"You sleep on the bed, Baby. I'll sleep on the sofa. Maybe I'll sleep with the redhead." He bent over and kissed her gently, then left the room.

A tear found its way down the side of her nose. It tickled a little, and she brushed it away. Something had died within her. The blood-stained face of the young man came before her eyes. Her heart beat slightly faster. A thought occurred to her. How could she ever allow Joe to touch her again—to make love to her? She went cold all over at the thought. Perhaps, if she had not seen that bloody face she would not feel this way now. What had possessed her to go to the shack—to stop the fight and to bring back the redhead? Suddenly her heart began to throb. It was so hard to concentrate. She fell asleep thinking of the young man driving by in his car. The shivers that tickled her spine were delicious. It was so much more pleasant this way. And her head didn't hurt any longer.

CHAPTER NINE

THE next morning was hot and muggy, as it had been all summer. Joe woke up stiff from his sleepless night on the sofa. An ordinary sized person might have been comfortable on it. The cheap upholstery was soaked with his perspiration. The Colella baby, next door, shrieked with a vigor replenished by sleep. The smell of frying eggs came to him.

Teresa had a batch of eggs in the frying pan. By the time he had washed and sat at the kitchen table, a platter was ready for him. It was just like any other morning. For a moment, he wondered who the tea and toast was for. Then he remembered the redhead.

"How's the redhead?" he asked.

"He is awake. He wanted to get up to cook breakfast for everyone. I did not let him, of course." She sounded as though everything was fine. She was serene and appeared to have forgotten the night before.

"You didn't ask me if I had a good night's sleep. That'll be the last time on that sofa for me, you can bet."

The girl was silent.

"Did you hear me, Baby?"

She nodded. "I am sorry. I guess I will have to sleep on the sofa, then."

"Hey, what is this? You mean, for always?"

"I am sorry, Joe. When I think of that young man with all that blood—" She shivered.

Joe, knowing the forgiving nature of the girl, felt that she would be over it in a day or two. "I'm sorry, Baby. We'll talk about it later." He got up from the table, went to the redhead's bedroom and opened the door.

"Hey, you ugly bastard," he called softly, "how do you feel, eh?"

The redhead grinned. He had washed and his brilliant red hair was slicked down with water. Joe had never seen him like this. "Not so bad, Joe. I feel pretty good. I feel like getting up and coming down to work with you."

"You heard the doctor. You got to get plenty of rest. So you stay right there, eh, Redhead. My Teresa will take good care of you."

"Okay, Joe."

"Well, I've got to go. So long, Redhead."

"So long, Joe. Oh Joe! Make sure my place is locked up, will you?"

"Okay. See you."

Joe went to Teresa who was at the sink. "Teresa, baby," he whispered.

Without turning, she offered him her cheek. Leaning over her back, he kissed it. His arms circled her waist. But she gently unwound them. Still without turning, she said, "You'll be late for work, Joe."

"So long, Baby," he said. He strode to the door and out on the porch. He didn't know whether to be angry with the girl or not. Oh well, he thought, she'll be over it by tonight.

Giovanni was already on his porch, his tee-shirt already showing a large, wet spot around his belt line at his back. "How's the redhead," he called over.

"Looks good to me. Looks better than Sam did last night."
They both laughed.

They met in front of Giovanni's gate and started down the
road to the quarry. "What's the matter with your kid?" asked Joe.
"Seems like he's always crying."

"I do not know, Joe. Maybe it is the heat."

"Nah. They don't feel the heat at that age."

"My Maria thinks it is *il male occhio.*"

"The over-looks. It could be."

"Yes. Everybody is always saying what a beautiful baby he
is. You know babies do not have any resistance against this evil."

"Why the hell don't you get the old woman? She'll know if
he's got them or not. And she'll get rid of them in no time."

"Maria went to look for *la vecchia* at her hut. But she could
not find her. She must have gone on one of her trips."

"You still think she goes to visit the spirits, eh, Giovanni?"

"I do not know, Joe. People do not disappear just like that for
weeks at a time, then comes back out of nowhere."

Joe shrugged his shoulders. They had reached the redhead's
shack. Joe checked the door. It was locked. All the pit men had
gathered though it was still some twenty minutes before starting time. There were grins on all their faces, as they recalled and
discussed the events of the night before.

"How do you feel, Joe?" each asked.

"I thought he was a softie. But he's plenty tough if he ain't
dead after that beating," said Joe.

"It is a good thing for him that your woman stopped you, Joe.
It would have been bad all around, if he died," commented one
of the men.

"You're right there," agreed Joe, proud of his woman.

They all agreed that Sam Roma had it coming to him. They
hoped he would be in the hospital for a month. Perhaps he would

be a different man when he came back. But their small futile hopes were short-lived. Up the road, a cloud of dust raised their fears.

"E' *il diavolo*," whispered Angelo. He made the sign of the cross on his forehead.

"Yes, it is the sonofabitching devil, himself," whispered another, quoting the redhead's favorite expression. They had recognized Sam Roma's car. Behind it came a police car. In a moment, Sam Roma and two policemen were in their midst. Sam's face was a swollen, purplish mass. His eyebrow and left side of his forehead was bandaged. "There's the bastard." Sam pointed Joe out.

"Oh! It's you, is it?" One of the policemen recognized Joe. "Haven't seen you in town in a long time, Joe. It's been kind of quiet, too, without one of your week-end brawls."

"Hello, Fred." Joe grinned. "I've been behaving lately. Figured I gave you boys enough trouble."

"We got to take you in, Joe."

"Got a warrant?"

"Yep."

"Let's go." Joe walked by Sam Roma, raised his hand as though to slug him, then scratched his head as Sam pulled away involuntarily. A ripple of laughter was quickly stifled, as the men saw the hate in the eyes of Sam Roma. He glared at them, and they knew that today would be a long, bitter one. It would be one that they would long remember. They watched in frozen silence, as Joe got into the police car. They watched hopelessly as it drove off.

"Okay, you guys." There was no mistaking the vicious intent in Sam Roma's voice. They turned and filed down the path to the pit.

CHAPTER TEN

TERESA saw the police car come then leave with Joe in it. He had waved to her, grinning as they went by. Somehow, she hadn't felt any anxiety. She hadn't even been surprised. Before last night she would have felt remorse for Joe. She would have felt helpless and alone. She would have felt something. Now, there was absolutely nothing. As though Joe were a complete stranger to her. Later, she spoke to the redhead.

"Your friend, Joe, has been taken by the police. I do not know what we will do now. I have a little money that we have saved. When that is gone, I do not know— I must go to see Joe. He will tell me what I should do."

The redhead looked at Teresa through red, shaggy eyebrows that seemed to half cover his eyes. She wore the cotton housecoat, and the outline of her body was visible in the bright rays of the sun that splashed through the window. The redhead guessed that she hadn't anything on underneath. At least, he liked to think so.

He took stock of the situation. All last night he had been thinking how fortunate he was to be here in the same house with Joe's woman. He had pictured himself in her arms—in bed with her. Of course, he would have to be careful with Joe around. But what the hell, Joe was gone—away to work, all day long. His lecherous old heart had pounded at his thoughts until he gasped at the pain. He had forced himself to think of other things.

Now, the news of Joe's arrest had left him troubled. Could he stay here with the woman, now that Joe was gone? Would she stay? Would Joe allow it? All these questions bothered him. "When are you going to see Joe?" he asked.

"I will go as soon as I get ready. Will they hold him long?"

"I don't know. If Sam presses charges, Joe might get from thirty to ninety days. It all depends on Sam."

"But it was this Sam who caused you to become ill. You will tell them, won't you?"

"Sure I will."

The girl turned to leave the room.

"Oh, by the way, Miss Teresa." He couldn't think of a more suitable title. She turned at the door.

"Yes?" she asked.

"Could you do something for me?"

"Yes."

"My suitcase at the shack. Could you get it for me? Everything I have is in it."

"I will get it," she said simply. She opened the door and left, closing it gently behind her.

Redhead lay back and stretched luxuriously. He let out a deep sigh of satisfaction. Somehow, the girl had not seemed at all worried or depressed about Joe's arrest. He had noticed it. He had been mildly shocked at first. But the more he thought of it, the better he liked it. It had been strange, though, how impersonal, she had been about him. And why had Joe slept on the sofa last night? How Joe could sleep on a sofa with a woman such as Teresa in the bed was beyond him.

What a body! he thought. He remembered that last glimpse of the girl as she left the room, the housecoat taut against her buttocks. It would be unfortunate if Joe were to be freed. He found himself hoping that Joe would get at least thirty days....

Sam Roma saw Teresa enter the redhead's shack. He left the men and hurried up the path out of the quarry pit. He entered the shack. After coming out of the bright sunlight, his eyes were momentarily blinded. For a split second he felt her softness as he groped about in the tiny room. His ribs ached from the pounding of his heart and he found it hard to breathe. He was aware of the clean, soap smell of her.

The girl recoiled at the contact. Accustomed to the dimness, she had recognized Sam Roma. She shivered, waiting for him to move; wishing she were somewhere else; wishing that he might accidentally touch her again. Sam was finally able to make her out.

"Hey!" he said appreciatively. "So you're Joe's woman?"

"Joe's in jail now," she said stupidly.

"Yeah, and he's going to stay there, too, if I can help it. What are you doing here?"

"I came to get Mr. Malancuni's bag. Some of his things are in it."

"How is he?" Sam was able to see the girl quite clearly now. She was backed against the stone wall of the shack. She looked frightened. Sam made conversation to relax her. She answered automatically, her eyes wide with fright.

"He is doing fine. He needs rest."

"By the way, I want to thank you for getting Joe off of me, last night."

"He might have killed you. I had to do something." Her voice trembled violently.

"Why were you so worried about him killing me?" Sam moved slowly around the small table that separated them until he was facing her.

"It would have been bad for Joe."

"Is that all you were worried about?"

"Yes." Her voice was barely a whisper. She trembled violently at his nearness. The room suddenly felt unbearably hot. She felt that she was suffocating. Sam Roma laughed silently. With a deliberate movement, he put his hands on her shoulders.

"No!" she whimpered. She looked at the handsome face, handsome despite the swelling and the bandages, and she was engulfed by a tender emotion that left her weak.

He drew her unprotestingly to him. She looked up at him, helplessly, her lips parted. He kissed her, letting his mouth mold itself about hers, and savoring the sweet taste of her. Her arms hung limply at her sides. Her legs felt like they would never hold her up. If only he would let her slip to the floor. She felt so weak. On the floor, she thought. On *the floor*. Her mouth became a living thing, no longer passive. She could stand it no longer.

A yell came from far away in the pits. Sam started, loosening his hold. It was something that needed his attention. The girl clutched at him desperately. "No! Do not go. Do not leave me," she gasped. Sam loosened his hold entirely, and she almost fell to her knees. He laughed loudly as he left the shack. He would have plenty of time to take care of her. He would see to that.

The girl remained, leaning on the table, until her strength returned to her legs. Her head throbbed, and she knew that she would have a headache. In a little while, she found the suitcase in the corner and left the shack. As she made her way slowly toward the house she remembered that she had wanted to ask Sam to let Joe off easily. Now, she realized shamelessly, that it did not matter.

The redhead sat up in the bed when Teresa came into the room. He noticed the tired, spent stoop of her shoulders. There was something about her now that had not been a part of her when she had left to get his bag. He sensed that something had happened to her in the meantime. Maybe she had been sickened at the sight of his shack. He realized, now, that it was slovenly when compared to the room here at Joe's house. Maybe he shouldn't have sent her. Maybe she had met Sam Roma and had become upset about him. She had his cheap, battered, old bag with her. She walked listlessly to the bed and put it down.

"Thank you," said the redhead.

"Do you want it here?" she asked.

"Yeah." She started to leave. "Wait," he said. He took a key from a string tied around his neck and opened it. She had come back to the bedside and looked on. He dumped out the few clothes in the bag. He tore loose a stitch in the lining and took out an envelope. He held it to her.

"What is this?" she asked. Suddenly she had forgotten the shack and Sam Roma. Like a child with a new toy she was only interested in the joy that it would bring.

"It's some money that I saved. Tell Joe, when you go to see him, that he can use it any way he wants. Maybe for a lawyer." He handed her the envelope.

She opened slowly, trying to imagine what it was, getting a thrill from it. She took out the neatly piled stack of bills of different denominations. She had never seen so many crisp dollar bills all at one time before. She was at a loss for words. In her dull mind, the money meant security while Joe was in jail. But she would have to ask Joe of course. The money could help him out, too. It seemed like an awful lot of money.

"Mr. Malancuni," she protested in spite of herself, "you will need this money yourself. You will need the doctor." She could feel the redhead's eyes looking at her as she had seen others do. And in spite of his ugliness, the goose-pimples crawled up her arms. Somehow, he did not look so very horrible today. She hoped that the redhead would not change his mind about the money.

"No, you keep it," he said. It will help to pay for the doctor, and you will need it until Joe gets out. I wish it was more."

"Very well, then. I will see if Joe needs it." She had an impulse to kiss him because he was so kind, but she shuddered at the thought.

"That's good. Are you going to see Joe now?" The redhead grinned. And now he wasn't at all ugly, thought the girl. You just had to get used to him.

"I will go to see Joe now. The doctor said that he would be here to see you sometime this morning. Do not get out of bed. I will leave the door open for him."

"Give my regards to Joe."

"All right, Mr. Malancuni. I am sure that Joe will be happy to hear that you have been so kind." She left, clutching the envelope into which she had returned the money. She did not know how much there was, but it was over a hundred dollars.

The redhead relaxed in the bed. He was quite satisfied with himself. He felt that Joe would appreciate the offer of the money and would surely allow him to remain at the house. Joe might get thirty days, maybe ninety, if he knew Sam Roma. More power to Sam Roma, he thought.

The day had been quiet up till now. But suddenly all hell broke loose as Maria next door began screaming at her brood. The new baby began to bawl. The redhead began to feel sorry for himself. Then he heard the Colella's twelve-year-old trying to calm the smaller children, and he smiled to himself. He had seen her that morning, across the way, in the room opposite his. He felt better. Life had never been so good. As a matter of fact, it was so good that he had even neglected to think of Mrs. Giambra.

It was going to be another scorcher. Already, his borrowed pajamas were damp with perspiration. He kicked the sheet from off his body and tried to doze off. When the doctor came, in a little while, he found the redhead in a good frame of mind, his condition improved.

CHAPTER ELEVEN

TERESA saw Sam Roma at the trial. From her seat she had an excellent view of his profile. All through the case her eyes were drawn as though by a magnet. It seemed as though she could not keep her eyes from him. And when he turned, occasionally, and glanced at her, momentarily, their eyes would invariably meet. The bum that started at the back of her neck, sent a delicious tremor down her spine. Never, in all her life, had she ever seen such a handsome man. With the bandages and the swelling gone, Sam Roma's handsome ruggedness was indeed quite noticeable in the small courtroom. More than one feminine eye had discovered him and appraised him.

Teresa could still feel his lips on hers. But most vividly, in her mind, was the curious reaction of her legs—how she had wanted only to slip to the ground. She had never felt that way before—with any man.

The judge heard Sam Roma's testimony; how he had gone to the quarry to check up on things. He had found the four men, including Joe Carato, drunk. And when he had reprimanded Jake Malancuni, the watchman, for allowing such goings on, Joe had attacked him. As he spoke, Sam kept touching the scar above his eye. He mentioned the fact that it would remain with him for the rest of his life.

Sam spoke in an even tone. He spoke carefully with proper pronunciation, as though being prompted by Cynthia. He was not at ease, however, and he perspired profusely from the strain. He mopped his face and neck quite often. He seemed relieved when he left the stand. He glanced fully at Teresa. Instead of the tiny semblance of a grin, his face was grim. At the moment, his only interest was in having Joe convicted.

The redheaded Jake came to testify in spite of the doctor's protest. Jake looked pale. And more than once he paused in his testimony and took a deep breath. "Excuse me, Judge," he explained, "the doctor said I should be in bed and not here." This happened after each pause, which occurred more and more often. Soon the crowd began to anticipate the explanation and it brought a ripple of laughter. The judge finally told him that the court was positive, by now, that he should have stayed in bed.

This brought a loud bit of laughter which the judge had not expected. He had meant to stop the reoccurrence of the redhead's explanation. But somehow, it had struck the crowd as an attempt by the judge to be humorous. And they had responded spontaneously. The judge banged his gavel hard to bring the court back to normal.

Joe had a long damning list of assaults on his record—all while under the influence of drink. The most he had gotten for any of these offenses was a night in jail until he sobered up. They had been mainly barroom brawls involving at least two or three others. Joe made it a point to tangle with more than just one opponent. As a result, he had made himself quite a reputation around the town.

It was a short trial. Everyone seemed in a hurry. They wanted only to end it all and get away to some cool place. The judge, however, was calm and deliberate in spite of the perspiration that rolled down his body under the heavy vestment.

"Ninety days," he said in a solemn tone. "And I hope that this will serve as a lesson to you, Joseph Carato."

Joe had a violent urge to rush across the courtroom and wipe the smirk from Sam Roma's face. He trembled with his feeling of hopelessness. He let himself be led away by the officer. Just as he went through the side door he gave Teresa and the redhead one last despairing look.

Outside the court-house, Sam pulled up his car and stopped at the curb in front of Teresa and the redhead. "Can I give you a lift?" he asked.

Teresa would have gone willingly had it not been for the redhead. She declined the invitation, and Sam didn't miss the I'd-like-to-but-can't look. He chuckled to himself. "Sorry about Joe," he said and drove off.

"That sonofabitch," muttered the redhead. Somehow, though, he didn't feel quite like that. Instead, he felt an intoxicating excitement at the thought that now, somehow, fate had caused him and the girl to be brought together. Joe was definitely out of the way for ninety days. It was more than he had dared hope for. So he cursed Sam Roma to hide his true feelings.

Back at the house, Mrs. Colella was the first to ask about Joe.

"I saw that Sam Roma drive by in his car just a little while ago. He looked very happy with himself. So I feel that things did not go so good for Joe."

"Joe got ninety days," said Teresa.

"That is too bad." Mrs. Colella shook her head. She saw the redhead, chalk white under his unruly mop of red hair. "Hey, *Capirosso*, you do not look so good."

"The doctor told me to stay in bed, but I figured I'd go to court." He shrugged his shoulders. "I didn't do Joe any good, and I didn't do myself any good."

"Well, at least you tried." Mrs. Colella consoled him. "But you better get right to bed. You look very sick."

"Yeah, I don't feel so good. I think I'll go now." He went into the house, and Teresa remained to talk to Mrs. Colella.

"What will you do now, Teresa?"

"I do not know. Mr. Malancuni looks very bad. I will have to take care of him. Joe said that it was all right to let him stay."

"What will you do for money?"

"Oh, we have saved some money. It will be enough to keep us. Mr. Malancuni has a little, too. We will manage until Joe gets out."

One of the Colella kids in the backyard began to cry. "Let me go," said Mrs. Colella. She scurried away.

Inside, the redhead undressed, put on his pajamas and got into bed. Since coming to Joe's house, he had learned to bathe daily and wear pajamas. Teresa had insisted on it. She had even gone out to buy him two pair. And he was very proud of them. They were the first he had ever worn.

Now, as he lay in the bed, he felt as though he had not an ounce of strength in his body. He felt awful. The strain of the trial had been entirely too much for him.

In the window across from his, the Colella twelve-year-old came into sight. She looked across into the redhead's room. She could not see him on the bed. She started to hum. Instantly, the redhead's head popped up. He looked across into the girl's room. She came into sight, briefly. She had taken off her dress and was in a slip. The redhead passed his tongue over dry bps. She reappeared again, wearing tight shorts that hugged her boyish thighs, and a flimsy halter that barely covered her bosom. While still in front of the window she proceeded to fold the edge of her shorts so that even more of her thighs were exposed, showing a ring of white untanned skin on each leg. The redhead was aware of the awakening of his own body. And the more he looked at the girl, from the safety of the shadows in his room, the more his weakness evaporated. The girl looked across once more, then left her room. Redhead heard the screen on the front porch slam, and he knew that she had gone out.

He wondered where she went every afternoon, dressed like that. The little bitching slut, he thought. Probably fooling around with those kids from the town. Must be. There was nobody her age on Quarry Road. Oh wait a minute, now. There was Johnny Rialo, son of Angelo. He was seventeen. He was a good-looking boy, too. So that's who it was. It never occurred to him that Johnny was working down in the pit at the moment; that Johnny had plenty of girls is own age in the town.

From that moment on, the redhead formed voluptuous pictures in his mind of the two together. And always in his mind, she wore the scanty shorts. And Johnny's fingers were always groping about the edge of the shorts, trying desperately, then successfully to get to the milk-white flesh beneath. Finally, the tearing off of the encumbering nuisance.

The shorts, from that moment on, became a symbol of her seduction at the hands of Johnny. He closed his eyes and he saw the boy with his hands inside the shorts. The shorts falling from slim virginal hips, discarded as useless at the moment of the clumsy, clutching fusion of the two young, eager bodies.

The redhead clutched at his heart. The pain was like a tearing, ripping knife thrust. He could feel the furious pounding of his heart.

"Teresa!" he called, thoroughly frightened. "Teresa!"

Teresa opened the door, her eyes questioning. "Is everything all right?" she asked.

"I don't feel so good. I'm all broke out in a sweat. And my heart is going crazy. Please get the doctor for me."

The girl brought a towel. "The trial was really too much for you. The doctor was right. You do not look well." For the first

A.R. DISPALDO

time since his coming, she wiped the perspiration from him. She unbuttoned his pajama tops and wiped his chest. The mat of orange-red hair on his chest was a soaked mass. It fascinated the girl and she stared, her eyes straying to a point where it disappeared into his pajama pants. She wiped automatically as she stared. Finally, she snapped out of it.

"I will get some water, and you must take your pill," she said. She left the room. The redhead pulled the sheet up around his chest. His heart was pounding less forcefully now. He must be careful.

The girl brought water. She looked at the area of his pajama pants. It was covered by the sheet. She helped him to raise his head, and he took the pill, drinking some water to wash it down. He looked gratefully at the girl when he finally lay back on the pillow. There was no desire in him at the moment. The girl, however, had had been left quite unnerved by the contact. She quickly left him, after promising to get the doctor....

Sam Roma wasn't hitting it off too well with Cynthia. She had refused to come to the trial. They had had a bitter argument over it. Actually, he hadn't wanted her there. Joe's woman undoubtedly would be there—and there might be complications. It might have spoiled his chances with the girl if Cynthia were there. Women were funny that way. However, he had pretended to be bitterly hurt. He accused her of not loving him; of not wanting to be at his side. She would not give in an inch, and he was grateful for once that she possessed such a stubborn streak.

Sam Roma was glad when work ended for the day. The trial had taken a good deal out of him. The argument with Cynthia the night before hadn't helped any. And neither had the hostile stares of the men. All day he had had the feeling that one of them was about to throw a rock at his head. It was several minutes before actual quitting time when he blew the whistle. He sighed with relief when he sagged into the seat of his car.

The Quarry Road continued right on into town. The last house in the community, of course, was Mrs. Giambra's. A quarter mile of road follows, with a thick wooded area on one side and an open meadow on the other. The first building of the town proper was the fire-house. This was seated on part of a lot that had been cleared and made into a ball-field. Across the road were several old farm houses. These were old frame buildings, probably the oldest in the history of the town. Beyond them, was the town itself. All together, it was a bare country half mile to the doctor's house.

It was opposite the ball-field that Sam saw Teresa walking toward town. She could have made a call from Mrs. Giambra's store, the only phone in town. But somehow she hadn't felt like calling with the woman looking on. Even in her dull mind, she could sense the hatred and jealousy that raged in the woman's breast. Mrs. Colella had told her of the curious sexual affairs of Mrs. Giambra and the redhead. It had been a hit and run affair, as she had called it. Also, in her short and widely spaced conversations with Mrs. Colella, she had learned of Mrs. Giambra's claim to Joe Carato.

Teresa could not understand how the homely woman could have claims on anyone. She certainly could not see or imagine Joe Carato making love to her. Now Mrs. Giambra and Mr. Malancuni; that was possible and even ideal. They were a good match. Then why hadn't the woman offered to take the redhead into her house. She had been there that night. There were so many things she did not understand. But she knew that Mrs. Giambra hated her.

Sam Roma slowed down and stopped the car when he came abreast of her. She had stopped when she recognized him, and she waited. Her body, however, did not react as it had done at the shack. In her mind was one thought: she had to get to the doctor for the redhead. Perhaps Mr. Roma would drive her there.

"Jump in," called Sam.

"Please, Mr. Roma. Will you drive me to the doctor's house? I must get him for Mr. Malancuni. He is very sick."

"Sure, jump in." Sam opened the door on her side, and she entered the car. There was an urgency in her movement.

"What's the matter with the redhead?" he asked.

"He looks very sick, and I must get the doctor."

"Lucky for me, too. I never get a chance to see you alone like this." He slowed the car down and pulled to the side of the road once more. It was at the end of the ball-field and deserted. He started to put his arms around her.

"Please, Mr. Roma!" Her voice rose slightly.

"Just for a minute." His hands grasped her shoulders and tried to draw her to him.

"Mr. Roma!" Her voice rose hysterically. "Please, the doctor."

Sam Roma was puzzled and getting angry fast. What the hell had gotten into the girl?

"Please, Mr. Roma. I must get the doctor for Mr. Malancuni. He is very sick."

What a one track mind she's got, thought Sam. She has to get the doctor, and nothing else matters. Maybe after she gets the doctor, it'll be different, he reasoned. He started the car up again, and soon they were at the doctor's house. He waited outside for her. Soon she and the doctor came out. She came over to the side of the car. "I will go back with the doctor," she said.

"Wait now! I'll take you back."

"Thank you, Mr. Roma. But I do not want to trouble you. I will go with the doctor." Before he could argue further, she had gotten into the doctor's car and they went off. Sam Roma was left scratching his head....

The redhead was feeling a lot better a week later. He feigned weakness, however, whenever the girl was near. This made the girl more concerned than ever. She helped him to get in and out of bed, and to sit up when she fed him. He began to anticipate her arms around him when she helped him; to feel her breasts pressed hard against him; and to feel her heart pounding when she did. He found excuses to have her near, and to feel her nearness. More than once, his hand had touched her body accidently. He had felt the recoil and tensing of her flesh the first time. Each succeeding time had made her less conscious of it. Until now, he held on to her, making it appear as impersonal as possible. He knew, for certain, that she wore nothing under the housecoat.

He had learned to let out long, anguished groans at every movement. At night when alone, he moaned loudly, making sure that the girl heard. She came to see what was wrong, usually wearing a flimsy nightgown. He would ask for water, or make some excuse so that she would have to turn on the light. Her body came through quite clearly in silhouette. And when the light was full on her, the round darkness of her breasts and the hardened tip of her nipples showed to advantage. Her partially revealed body fascinated him. He usually felt worse after she came.

"You must rest," she would insist.

"But I've got to get back to work," he would say dejectedly.

"The job will wait." She would tuck him in, leaning over him, her breasts barely confined in the loose nightgown.

All his reposing moments were spent in the planning of the girl's seduction. Sparking the flame that burned in him were the occasional glimpses he got of the Colella girl as she prepared for bed and when she arose in the morning. And even when he did not actually see her, simply hearing her moving about—the rustle of her clothing as she dressed or undressed—stirred his blood. Twice, he had caught glimpses of her bare breasts as she flitted across the window opening. The girl's immature body whetted his appetite for Teresa and her more mature body.

In all of his sixty-odd years, Redhead didn't know himself exactly how old he was. He had seen and known many women. They had been short, abrupt affairs. Whenever he had felt the need, he had immediately found a woman. Any woman. It hadn't mattered too much whether she had been thin or fat, tall or short. He couldn't be choosy. When his needs were satisfied, he had left, with no feeling of any kind. There was no remorse or shame or compassion. It was done. He paid and left, satiated until the urge was felt once more.

Now, in the twilight of his life, the urges were infrequent— and they had been easily satisfied by Mrs. Giambra. There had been a physical understanding between these two; a complete and perfect understanding.

It was different now, with Joe's woman. He had allowed the urgency of his need to store up in his mind and in his body. Each touch of her, each glance, all gathered and amassed until finally the need had become over-powering.

So it was almost six weeks later, six weeks since Joe had been convicted that the redhead could stand it no longer.

He had planned and schemed for weeks. Several plans had come to mind. All seemed inadequate because he did not dare. He could get her drunk as he did the widow Giambra. Or he could grab her as she helped him in the bed. He thought of getting into her bed with her after she had fallen asleep. Suppose she screamed? The first plan seemed the best. But he had to get some wine first. She certainly wouldn't buy any. The doctor had forbidden it.

He felt that his time was running out. He could not pretend any longer. His body was getting sore from lying in bed so long. He had to get up and back to work. Outside, the early September nights were getting cooler. He could not wait much longer. He had to go out now so that his body could become acclimatized to the changing fall weather. It would go hard on his body if he started working in freezing weather. His old bones would never endure it.

He had better get done with the business at hand. He certainly would never feel any better for the task at hand.

Across the way, the Colella household had grown still. The only sounds were those of a lone cricket and a distant train that was barely audible as it chugged on its westbound way. He had seen the Colella girl again, earlier in the evening. She had been fully dressed, and it had not bothered him in the least.

What the hell, he thought. That little teaser could get a guy into trouble. Let that little snotnose Johnny take care of her. Besides, there was Teresa in the next room. She was ready. It was a long time for a woman to be without a man. Especially a woman like Teresa. There was no doubt about it. She was ready.

And although the redhead was merely guessing at Teresa's mental and physical state, it was a fact that she was ready, as the redhead put it. She had begun to regard him with a look other than that of a nurse for a patient. It seemed that in the last two weeks she had been unable to keep her eyes from his body. She was fascinated by his large, gnarled hands and long muscled arms and ugly face.

The long siege in bed had caused him to lose his tan and his face was pasty, accentuating the brightness of his red hair. His pale blue eyes contrasted sharply in this strange combination that nature had concocted. Her stares had become bolder, lingering. His hands on her, when she helped him, sent tiny shivers through her. Her hands lingered on his body, and there was a new agonized look that came more often with each passing day.

In the next room, Redhead could hear the girl's restless movements. It had been that way for almost a week now.

Teresa sat before the large, gilded mirror that hung on the wall over the stained vanity. She stroked her hair, letting it spill over her neck and shoulders like a dark shadow. Her face wore a pensive look of dejection. She was very, very unhappy. She wondered what was happening to her. She was so uncertain, so helpless. Her reflection showed her face, peaked and drawn. Her body had lost none of its fullness, but there was the hint of a sag about her shoulders.

Joe had told her only yesterday, "You ain't looking so good, Baby. You look like you need a lot of loving. And I'll sure make it up to you when I get out."

She had smiled wanly, saying nothing.

"By the way, how is the redhead?" he had asked.

"He is feeling much better. He has told me that he will leave the house soon, and go back to the quarry."

"You tell him to stay as long as he wants. You hear? Tell him to stay until I get out, anyway, eh, Baby."

"I will tell him.

"You sure he ain't too much trouble? Maybe, that's why you look so tired," said Joe anxiously.

"No. He is no trouble. I feel fine."

"You're sure now, Teresa?" Then with a laugh. "You better watch the old redhead, though. If he starts to feel better, you're liable to find him in your bed some night. "

Teresa had crimsoned, and Joe had cut his joking short. Then with a more soothing tone, "I'll be out soon, Baby. Then everything will be right again."

"I will wait," she answered simply.

She thought of the visit as she stroked her hair, making it glisten luxuriously. Nothing made any sense anymore. Especially what was happening to her.

She didn't love Joe. Of this, there was no doubt in her simple mind. Her visits left her cold, without feeling. She only went because she felt that she owed it to him. If it weren't for the fact that she were still living in his house, she doubted if she would go at all. It had been this way since Sam Roma had come into her muddled life.

Now, even as she thought of him, her legs jelled. She felt the delicious chill that she had felt at the shack. That, however, was the only memory that she had of him through all these weeks. She watched for him as he drove to and from the quarry. He drove by without even a sideward glance. And each time she saw him, her stomach crawled and was sick with despair. The pounding of her heart suffocated her. She felt a hurt that she could not understand.

Why didn't he look? Why didn't he come and take her into his arms and kiss her like he had done before? What had she done? Surely, it couldn't be because of the night she had gone to get the doctor. Didn't he understand how urgent it was for the doctor to visit the redhead? Couldn't he understand? If only she could explain to him. She wanted to, so much.

"Sam, Sam!" she wailed, suddenly, softly. She pressed her legs together, hard, to ease the pleasant ache in thighs. "Sam Roma," she said softly, wonderingly. She had never said his name before, and it sounded so beautiful. "Sam, Sam! she said over and over again. "Oh Sam," she wailed. A tear rolled down the corner of her eye. She wiped it from the bridge of her nose with her knuckle. What was she to do? Her body felt so useless, so dead. It missed the lusty, vigorous assaults of Joe Carato upon it. It missed the coarse hands that made her skin bum and grow alive as her blood reacted and made her body pink, flushed with excitement.

It had been so long, now, since her body had been roused, and it ached and clamoured, seeking release.

"Sam, Sam," she cried softly.

Through the thin partition, she heard the restless movements of the redhead. Just as she had listened night after night, as she had waited for his moan, so that she could go to his room. Tonight, her body responded exultantly to the sound. Her bosom grew taut, her nipples hardening. Suddenly, she did not feel the necessity of brushing her hair. She gave two more swift, impatient strokes and put the brush aside. She listened intently, straining to hear more sounds. She heard the rustle again, a moan.

She arose from the seat, went to the light switch and turned off the light. For a moment, she saw nothing until she became accustomed to the darkness. Slowly she took off her nightgown. Her body burned, feeling weightless. She opened her door and walked into the hallway. The redhead's door was open, inviting. The redhead's eyes shone in the darkness like a huge cat's, watching her. Her body glistened and made soft, warm shadows.

"What is wrong? Why do you moan, so?" she asked softly.

"It's nothing. It's only because it is so hot."

"Then I must help you to take these off. You will be more comfortable." She leaned over him and began to help him off with his pajama tops. Then his bottoms. And even as she undressed him, his hands fondled her. Her skin burned under his touch. Finally, she threw the pants into a corner and lay down on the bed. As though it were a signal, the redhead became as one crazed. His lips burned and bruised her body, returning time and again, to the sweetness of her breasts.

She lay passive, letting his horny hands and his burning lips arouse wave after wave of passion in her, letting the waves build up until they became one overwhelming tidal wave that tore at her insides. The savage, brutal face of the redhead swam over her, and suddenly her body responded like the tides. All the pent impassioned weeks of privation found violent release.

She lay still, her body at peace. The redhead lay beside her, panting and wheezing. After a short while, he grew silent. She got up out of the bed. Her body felt once more like her own. Looking at the redhead, now, she recoiled at his ugliness. She covered him with the sheet, then returned to her own room. She fell asleep quickly, exhausted.

CHAPTER TWELVE

THE twelve-year-old Colella girl awoke with her mother's voice ringing in her ears.

"Come on, you. You will be late for school again!"

The girl lay in bed for a moment, her eyes barely open. They popped open, suddenly. She leaned over, taking care not to disturb her younger sister, and peeped over the sill into the redhead's room. She usually caught him looking over into her room in the mornings. The redhead wasn't looking this morning. He lay still in his bed.

"*Si fa tardi,*" yelled Mrs. Colella. "You will be late."

The girl recalled the strange noises of the night before—like the noises that came out of poppa and momma's room. It puzzled her. She knew what the noises were. The kids in school always talked about it, about how babies were made. She giggled. Who would want to do that with the ugly redhead?

She saw Teresa come into the redhead's room. She always looked so pretty but sad. This morning, she looked happy.

"Mr. Malancuni," she heard her say softly. "Are you ready for breakfast?"

There was no answer from the bed. The girl saw Teresa go to the bed. She shook the redhead gently. "Mr. Malancuni! Wake up. You have to take your medicine." The redhead remained inert, the head tilted slightly. Teresa shook him again, a little more forcefully his time. The head rolled grotesquely.

Teresa screamed. She screamed again and again. The girl's sleeping little sister awoke and began crying. The girl's heart pounded furiously. She ran out to the kitchen. Mrs. Colella had remained at the gas range, a fork poised in mid-air in the act of scrambling a pair of eggs.

"Mom, Mom!" screamed the girl. "Something's happened to the redhead." The screams had ceased. Suddenly, their entrance door burst open. It was Teresa, white faced, eyes wild with fear.

"Mr. Malancuni," she said in a tiny voice. "I think he is dead."

Maria Colella was used to death. She had lost two children herself. She remained calm.

"Go get your father, you. *Fai subito–Go* quick," she said to her daughter. The girl rushed to her room. She returned in an instant, wearing a faded pair of dungarees. She rushed out of the house. All of the Colella brood was crying and screaming by now. Teresa sat down weakly, staring into Mrs. Colella's calm face. Her mind flew back to her childhood; to the little store and Schultzie.

"You mustn't say anything to you mother, or you will be punished," he had told her. It had long since faded from her memory. She remembered it vividly now.

"It wasn't my fault," she murmured. "I did not make him die."

"Of course it is not your fault, Teresa. He was sick and he died. *Era la volonta' di Dio.* It was God's will."

Teresa turned wild eyes at the older woman. "No! They will blame me. They will punish me. I know they will punish me. Oh, if Joe were only here!"

"Do not worry," Mrs. Colella snapped impatiently. "It is not your fault. They will not do anything to you."

From Joe's house came the babble of many voices. All of the people of the community had gathered. Some of the crowd had started to overflow into the Colella home along with Giovanni.

"What happened?" he asked his wife.

"I do not know. Teresa tried to wake him up this morning, and she found him dead."

"That's right, Poppa. I saw everything through the window."

Giovanni turned to his daughter, and she shrank under the terrifying look he gave her. "You go to school, you hear." She ran to her room. From the shadows, she looked across at the milling crowd that had found its way to the redhead's room. Two women kneeled in prayer beside the bed. She recognized Mrs. Giambra, the store-keeper. The woman took one look at the body, still in the same position that she had last seen it, and she walked away. Could it have been a shudder that made Mrs. Giambra shake like that.

In the living room, Teresa sat, her head bowed. "I did not do it, " she whispered over and over again. "It was not my fault." And the good people of Quarry Road shook their heads and whispered silent prayers for the soul of the departed.

The whispering silence was broken by Mrs. Giambra who burst into the house. She stood over the bowed head of the weeping girl like an avenging angel and screamed foul names and vile insinuations. "You are evil. Witch! First Joe Carato, now the redhead. Who will be next?"

"It was not my fault," moaned the girl.

Mrs. Giambra turned to the Colellas. "She is evil. Get her from this house before she brings evil to you and your family!" Her voice rose hysterically. The women in the crowd made the sign of the cross.

Giovanni took the wild woman by the shoulders and shook her. "You talk like a wicked old woman. It is nobody's fault. He was a very sick man. Now, calm down." He led her toward the door. "Go home and call the police. They will take care of the body." He pushed her gently through the door. "All right, now." He turned to the crowd. "You can all go home." One by one, they filed past Teresa, her head still bowed like a penitant child. In their small, righteous peasant minds, the seed had been planted.

It was true, what Mrs. Giambra had said. Ever since the woman had come to five with Joe terrible things had happened; things that had been happening all their lives and never needed explaining. Now they took on new meaning. Joe's fight and arrest; the death of the redhead—both seemed suddenly to hold a new significance. Both incidences were close to the girl. Had it happened to any other person on the Road it would have been a coincidence. But the girl was an outsider. Mrs. Giambra was right.

Now, the good people gathered outside the house and whispered among themselves. It was the work of an evil one, they agreed. When the police came, accompanied by an ambulance, the crowd streamed out of Joe's house. They joined the rest outside, and there was more whispering. Giovanni took the girl back to Joe's house. When they saw her they glanced at one another furtively. There were scared faces, anxious faces. Who would be next, they wondered. Who would the evil eye fall on next? They waited around until the body was taken away.

CHAPTER THIRTEEN

SAM ROMA kissed Cynthia good night. It was a cool, short kiss—strictly good night. It left Sam cold and empty inside. He got into his car and drove off. It had been that way for a week now, since the redhead's death. Without even thinking about it, he headed toward the quarry.

He had been unable to get Joe's woman out of his mind. Each night, after leaving Cynthia, he had automatically headed in that direction. Always at a late hour, the community was asleep. It might have been deserted, it was so dark and quiet. He had fought the urge to go to the door and knock, to wake the sleeping Teresa, to kiss her drowsy lips and feel her awaken to passion. He envisioned her coming to the door, her body still warm, and her eyes, heavy-lidded. She would be wearing a thin gown, her bosom barely hidden. Her bps would be moist, ready for his kiss. They would be sweet without lipstick.

He had hated himself from the very day when he had let the opportunity slip away from him. The day he had kissed her in the shack. She had been so completely ready to submit. He still remembered the feel of her thighs as she sagged against him, how she had begged him to let her slip to the floor of the filthy shack. Sam could feel the blood thickening in his veins.

He wondered how he had let so much time pass before attempting to see the girl. Actually, he had thought about her often. Somehow, Cynthia had managed to keep him busy—dangling on her golden string. She had been warmer than usual. Warmer and more tender than she had ever been. Sam had been content with the promise she gave with her lips and her cool seductive body that she had such masterful control over. That had helped keep him away from Joe's woman. The other reason was gone now. Redhead was dead, and there was nothing to stop him now.

The girl was all alone for the taking.

He looked at the clock on the dashboard. Twelve-thirty. He turned into Quarry Road, passed the firehouse and slowed down to a crawl. He drove slowly down the quarter mile stretch of road before reaching the small group of houses. They were dark outlines in the dim moonlight. Fifty feet ahead, he distinguished Mrs. Giambra's store on the corner. All the houses were dark. Quarrytown was asleep.

He pulled to the curb and turned off his ignition and headlights. He lit a cigarette and sat back. He would smoke it, trying to muster enough nerve to knock on her door. Maybe it would be better to go in the daytime. He could go and ask if she needed any help now that she was alone. It might be better that way.

Suddenly, a lone window grew bright. It stood out sharply against the surrounding darkness. He licked his lips that had suddenly gone dry. His stomach lurched. He sat motionless, uncertain of himself. Was it her light? Should he chance it? Suppose he was seen?

He got out of the car and leaned against the fender. He became aware of the night sounds. A cricket chirped almost underfoot, making him jump. If only he could be sure it was her light. He began walking slowly toward the light. Without realizing it, he reached Mrs. Giambra's store. The light shone from a window in the next house.

Joe's house.

He remained rooted to the spot in the shadows of a white-barked elm. He found it hard to breathe, and his stomach felt tight. He sucked air hard and deep. It made him feel better. What the hell's the matter with me, he thought. Never felt like this with a dame before.

The light went out He walked silently up the walk and onto the porch. He knocked on the door with quick short raps, then moved off to the side into the shadows. He licked his lips nervously. It was one thing to stand up to Joe Carato, even knowing full well that he was in for a beating. But to invade the home of these people—to take his woman. He was one of them. He knew what it meant. For this offense, there was only one end result—killing was too good. There was nothing else that could save a man's respect.

The door opened a crack. Sam realized it only by the soft sound of the latch being released. The house remained dark.

"Who is it," he heard her whisper.

He stepped into the moon-lit area in front of the door. Immediately, the door opened wide enough to let him slip through. He brushed against her, feeling the warm dampness of her, feeling her softness as he had in the shack.

The door closed behind him and they remained, the two of them in the darkness, unbelieving. In its safety Sam felt the butterflies leave his stomach. Without touching her, he could feel her presence. He breathed in deeply the clean body smell of her. Cynthia always smelled of the fragrance of perfume.

"I had to get a glass of water," she whispered, not sure of what to say. He reached out into the darkness and found her naked shoulders, soft and fragile in his strong hands. He felt her body going limp.

"I'm glad you did," he whispered. He drew her to him. In the darkness he found her lips quite easily. A soft sound formed in her throat. Her arms crept around his waist, her thighs grinding against him.

"It is cold here," she giggled, happily.

"Where's the bed," he gasped.

She disengaged herself, and there was a frenzied urgency in her movements. "Come quickly," she said. She took his arm. He followed her, groping his way through a doorway. Then, he saw her. The moon shone full on the bed. She sank on it. The pale light left nothing to his imagination. The nightgown had drawn up on her thighs. Her heavy lids opened slightly.

"Hurry," she whispered. "Hurry to me."

He could not keep his eyes from her body, as he frantically tore at his clothes. She pressed her legs together, once. Then they spread again, ever so slightly. She saw his strong slim body. She stretched out her arms to him. He took her hands and pulled her up until she was standing beside the bed. The gown had slipped down over her body.

"Now take it off," he ordered.

She pulled the hem up over her head until it was all off. Her upraised arms caused her ample bosom to thrust upwards. Sam could stand it no longer. He grabbed her around the waist and lifted her so that his face was buried in the softness of her moist breast. The girl's arms wrapped themselves about his head and almost smothered him. They fell to the bed.

Sam Roma was rough in his love-making, as rough as Joe had ever been. He bruised her body with his rough hands, and his kisses made her lips swollen and sore. But the pain had never been so exquisite.

"I love you! I love you!" The words of love came easily from her lips. It had never been so easy for her to utter them in her life. When her body had been given release, the way she had never dreamed possible, she kissed his face with tender gratuitous kisses. And she dared to whisper his name.

"I love you, Sam. I love you so much."

He kissed her mouth. "I love you too, Teresa," he whispered into her mouth. He said it automatically, feeling that he should. It had been good. There was no denying it. He had never in his life encountered such pent passion as she possessed. And she withheld nothing from him. She now lay passive, thanking him with her sweet kisses. They lay like that for a time, the girl's hands exploring the muscles of his arms and back, as though she could not get over the wonder of his body.

They had been silent for some time. Finally Sam started to get up. She held him close. "I've got to go now, Teresa."

"Please do not go yet," she whispered. She pulled his head to her breast, twisting her body until his lips found a hard, swollen crest. And he stayed while the passion mounted again.

It was much later when she let him out at the front door. "You will come again?" she whispered.

"You bet."

"Tomorrow night?"

"I don't know."

"Please !" She pressed her body against him.

"Okay."

"I will wait for you."

"Okay," he said, really anxious to get away. "You wait for me."

"Kiss me." Her breast and thighs were soft and alluring beneath her nightgown. Suddenly, he began to feel panicky. He wanted to get away before someone saw him. He kissed her quickly and walked out into the cool night. Once beyond Mrs. Giambra's store, he ran to his car. He drove almost to the firehouse before he turned on the headlights of his car. He had to wipe the cold perspiration from his brow in spite of the cool night....

It was several weeks later. The Colella household was still. The Colella brood was asleep. Maria Colella lay on her back, wondering if she were pregnant again. When will it stop? She turned her head and looked tenderly at Giovanni. She saw that he was wide awake, staring at the ceding.

"Giovanni," she whispered, "why do you not sleep?"

"It is nothing, *cara mia*. Go to sleep."

"Something troubles you. Do you worry that I am pregnant again?"

"No, *earn*. I do not worry, if you do not worry."

"I do not, Giovanni *mio*. I will welcome as many as God wills, as long as you are the father."

"*Cara* Maria," he said, then fell silent.

Maria said nothing. It was times like this, when they lay in bed, that they were in accord; when they lapsed into the occasional Italian phrases of endearment; when they poured their hearts out to one another. She waited. She knew that he would need no coaxing, that he would tell her what was on his mind. She waited patiently, loving him.

"Maria," he whispered finally.

"Yes, Giovanni."

"Are you awake?"

"Yes."

There was a short pause. "Teresa came to the quarry today. She came to her lover. She came like a tramp to see Sam Roma."

"Sam Roma!" Maria gasped.

"Yes, Sam Roma. And they fight like lovers."

"No, Giovanni. You must be mistaken."

"I wish to God that I am. They fight. Sam does not want her there. But she will not go away. She wants to know why he does not come for three nights. I hear everything. Then he says, okay I see you tonight—and she goes away. Everybody hears them."

"Poor Joe," whispered Maria.

Giovanni's voice was bitter. "To take one's woman in his own house! Joe will surely kill him—this time."

"What will he do to the girl?"

Giovanni let out a long sigh. "I do not know," he said finally. "If he does not break her pretty neck, no one will be surprised. And if he does, no one will be surprised. Joe will hate her for what she has done, but he loves her more."

"What you say is true. She is such a child in her mind. She does not realize that she does wrong. I feel so sorry for her," said Maria pityingly.

There was a long silence in the room. Then Maria heard the soft snoring of Giovanni, and she knew that his mind was unburdened; he had told her his troubles, which were not really his troubles, and now he slept. And she loved him all the more for it.

"*Ti amo*," she said softly. But to her sleep did not come so easily. She arose from the bed and went to the tiny crib where the baby slept. She leaned over and kissed it gently. It stirred with a start then settled itself and slept comfortably. In the next room, only large enough for one double bed, her three small boy children slept in a tangle of arms and legs. They all slept soundly in spite of the awkward positions they had assumed. She saw them and smiled, and she covered them as best she could. She knew that they would all be uncovered before long.

She went finally into the other bedroom. Her twelve-year old slept like a little lady, her legs curled ever so slightly under the covers. The four-year-old girl cuddled against her back, seeking the warmth from the older girl's body. Maria looked long at her first born. She saw the budding breasts that were easily confined against the thin cotton nightgown. Soon they would be full and they would provide nourishment for Maria's grandchildren. Soon the girl, sleeping so peacefully, would be a woman. She would have children of her own. God only knew what was in store for her; the suffering she would have to endure before the good Lord took her back to him.

Across the areaway, the room where the redhead had slept looked dark and lonely and empty of life. Perhaps the spirit of the redhead still lurked there. Maria shivered and made the sign of the cross. God forgive her, he had been ugly enough in life. She left the room, leaving the door open.

Somehow, sleep did not come so easily tonight. She wandered about the dark house, avoiding the dim outlines of the old furniture. She continually found her way back to the side window that faced Joe's house. She looked across. It was dark and still. Finally she lifted one of the kitchen chairs and brought it silently to the window. She sat down and waited, her eyes staring at the porch across the yard.

Maria Colella was genuinely sorry for Teresa. She knew how a woman could feel without the arms of a man about her, to feel the gentle release that only a man's body could bring to a woman. She had felt the vacancy many times. With each of her children, there had come a time when it was impossible for Giovanni to touch her—when she had wanted him so terribly much that she had cried herself to sleep. She had known what it was like. And she pitied Teresa and forgave her.

It wasn't long before she saw the lurking figure walking stealthily up the walk, and, without knocking, go into the house. There was no mistaking the straight, slim figure of Sam Roma.

CHAPTER FOURTEEN

MARIA waited until she saw Teresa moving about the next morning before she went over. Teresa seemed as happy and as bubbling as a new bride. She greeted Maria with a big hug and proceeded to pour coffee. Maria never refused coffee. But today she toyed with her cup and remained silent as she watched Teresa's beaming face. The girl looked so beautiful in her happiness. Maria began to wish that she hadn't come. Why had she come, anyway? Surely, this was no business of hers. Teresa was truly happy. Could this be wrong, if she was so happy? Maria stared, not knowing what to say or do.

Finally, Teresa looked at her with the face of a happy child—like her own twelve year old, she thought.

"Something troubles you, Maria," she said simply.

Maria could say nothing. She just stared.

"Please do not be so sad, Maria. For I am so happy that I am afraid I will surely burst."

"Why are you so happy, Teresa?" Maria did not know whether to expect a lie or not.

"Maria, Sam Roma has told me that he will marry me."

Maria was stunned at the girl's frankness. It was sinful to be so truthful. "But I do not understand." It was all she could say. She had come to scold her, to make her realize what she was doing was wrong. What could she say now?

"It is simple," said Teresa. "It is really very simple, and it is the most beautiful thing that has ever happened to me. It is as it was when you fell in love with Giovanni."

"Oh, my poor, sweet Teresa." Maria felt like crying. It had been so long since she had cried.

"Sam Roma has been coming to me for almost a month now. Ever since the redhead died. And I am so very much in love with Sam."

Maria shook her head incredulously. "But Joe—what about Joe?" And instantly she wished that her tongue had been cut off. For Teresa's face seemed to fall apart. The happiness that had suffused it faded and she stared in bewilderment.

"Joe?" she muttered. "But I do not love Joe. I never loved him. He was kind to me. I stayed with him, and cooked his meals, and I made him happy. But only because he was so good to me. I did not love him."

"But Joe loves you," said Maria. "Have you told him yet?"

"No."

"He will kill Sam Roma."

"Oh, no!" Teresa whimpered. "No! He must not. I do not understand. For the first time in my life, I am happy with love. What is wrong? Why is it that I cannot marry him? And why should Joe wish to kill him?"

"Perhaps it is better that you do not understand these things," said Maria. "Listen to me. You must do as I tell you." Maria's heart went out to this poor helpless girl. At least she could give her some advice.

"Teresa, do you listen to me?"

The girl nodded.

"You must go to the jail where they have Joe. You must tell him everything. Perhaps he is so much in love with you that he will give you his blessings. But if he is angry, then you must go away with Sam Roma. You must go far away. Do you understand me, Teresa? You must go so far away that Joe will not find you. For if he does, he will surely kill you both."

"Perhaps if I tell him that I am to have Sam Roma's baby—he will forgive me." The thought brightened Teresa's features.

"You would lie to him?"

"I do not think it is a lie."

Maria put her hand to her forehead in disbelief. "*Madonna mia*," she said. "You are *inciento?*"

"I think so. This morning, I vomited upon awaking. I think that is the way women know. Is it not so?"

"It is so." Maria was very familiar with the feeling. "Does Sam Roma know of this?"

"No."

"And he has promised to marry you?"

"He swore that he would as we lay in bed."

Maria shook her head at the simplicity of this child-woman. God help you, she thought. For she knew of Sam Roma and Cynthia Cavalla, as did everyone else from the quarry. And she knew of the promises that a man will make when his blood is hot with passion.

"Yes," she said, "you must tell Joe of the baby. I think it will make Joe feel different." She rose from the table, her coffee still untouched. Suddenly something stirred within her. She kissed Teresa on the forehead. And Teresa clung to her.

"You must go to Joe and tell him today. I think he will understand." Then she left....

At Mrs. Giambra's store, later in the day, Mrs. Giambra greeted Maria with that superior look of the righteous that Maria had learned to loathe. And she knew that Mrs. Giambra had also stayed awake last night.

"It seems that I was wrong, Maria. I thought your Giovanni would be next on her list. But I see that it is Sam Roma."

"What do you mean?" asked Maria, innocently.

"You do not have to lie to me," gloated Mrs. Giambra. "I saw Sam Roma sneaking into Joe's house last night. And she went by my store today to see Joe. And you know, she looked like there was nothing wrong with what she was doing. She goes to visit him still." She paused for breath. "I hope Joe breaks her skinny neck when he gets out." There was no pretense in her voice now. She spit out the words between clenched teeth.

Maria could stand her vicious tongue no longer. "Mrs. Giambra, if that girl would live to be a thousand years old, she could never cause all the trouble you have caused here with your vile tongue. You are nothing but a troublesome, wicked old woman. You hate this poor girl because of her youth, because she has taken what you think belongs to you." Maria paused, but only for a moment. "Do you think that Joe would ever have you, even if he did not have Teresa. Even the Redhead would not have you, unless you got him so drunk that he did not know what he was doing."

Mrs. Giambra remained speechless, for once. Her thin lips parted in amazement. Never before had anyone told her of her shortcomings to her face. And before she could summon up a tart remark, Mrs. Colella had picked up her bag of groceries and had left the store....

The county jail was a comparatively new building near the center of town. It was easily recognizable. It was the only one story building along the main street, and it was built along modern lines. The other buildings were some thirty years older, and the difference in architecture was obvious. The stores that lined the street were merely large show-windows and a doorway to one side. No imagination had gone into their designing. Even the bank on the corner was of the style prevalent in the first World War era. It was built solidly of huge granite blocks. It gave the townspeople a feeling of security, a good, safe place to put their savings.

The desk sergeant stopped talking to a young rookie cop when Teresa came through the entrance door of the jail. "Here comes big Joe Carato's woman again," he said out of the corner of his mouth. The rookie cop just stared as she came up to the desk. She smiled shyly. The sergeant smiled back broadly.

"I would like to see Joe Carato. He is in the jail here," she said.

"Yes, Ma'm." He scribbled on a pad, tore off the sheet, and handed it to her. "Go through that door, and the jailer will take care of you."

"Yes, I know. Thank you." She walked away, her hips swaying ever so slightly, just enough to fire the imagination. The two policemen stared after her.

"I sure would like to take care of her," said the young cop grinning.

"I guess you would," agreed the sergeant. "So would every other guy in this town, from six to sixty. The only reason nobody's tried anything, I guess, is because they'd have to tangle with big Joe."

"What's he in for?" The young cop was new on the force.

"Assault. He almost killed some guy. And for practically no reason at all. I'd hate to see him tangle with some guy over his woman."

"Oh, well," said the rookie, "I guess I'll have to be satisfied to take it out on the old lady." He grinned.

"Yeah. It's healthier that way."

In the visiting room Joe met Teresa with an ugly unshaven scowl. "Where the hell have you been all this time? I've seen you once since the redhead died." He gripped the grill that separated them and pushed his face hard against it. Teresa stared, her eyes wide in surprise. She was not prepared for Joe's violent display of temper. And for a moment, she was at a loss for words.

"I was at home always," she whispered lamely.

"You must have been pretty busy, all by yourself," Joe said sarcastically.

Teresa's eyes searched his for some sign. Joe had never even raised his voice to her. And now she was frightened. "I am sorry, Joe. I did not think about it."

Joe melted. He looked at the frightened girl, and all the pent-up anger that had boiled in him for days suddenly was released from his system by a low chuckle. "Hyah, Baby," he said grinning.

"Hello, Joe." Teresa saw the change and she smiled with relief. "How do you feel?"

Joe was himself once more; carefree, gruff but tender. "Baby," he said grinning, "I feel like a tiger. I can't wait until I get out of here. I owe you plenty of loving."

"Please, Joe. Do not talk like that." The girl looked nervously at the jailer. He grinned at her from a chair within hearing distance.

"I can't help it. Baby. It's all I think about. I'll be out in a month, and I'll make it up to you. You see if I don't."

Teresa saw the expectations and desire in Joe's face. She became confused. And with the confusion came fright. How could she tell him of Sam Roma now. He would be so terribly angry. Perhaps, if she didn't tell him—he wouldn't get angry if he did not know. And with her limited reasoning, it solved every-thing. The future and what was in store was obscured; it did not matter. For the time being, and that was the important thing to her, his ignorance solved everything. Something would surely happen in the meanwhile.

She smiled up at him, and she was glad that she hadn't hurt him. She felt contentment in the knowledge that she had given him no cause for mental anguish. Not telling him the truth and the possibility of hurting him later and the consequences did not occur to her.

"I need you, Baby," he said tenderly.

"I am glad, Joe." There was a genuine gladness in her voice. Joe smiled at her. Somehow, he felt all choked up inside. That this tiny, helpless woman of his should stick by him, even though he had let her down, was hard to believe. He did not deserve such a woman. As he looked at her slight but well rounded figure, at her bosom that fought confinement, his emotions changed perceptibly. His voice grew husky and thick.

"Baby, I can't wait," he whispered.

"You must be patient."

"Just say the word, and I'll tear these bars apart." Joe was grinning, teasing.

"No! No, Joe! You will get in trouble." Teresa was truly alarmed.

"Okay, Baby," Joe continued grinning.

"Time's up, Joe," yelled the jailer.

"Okay, Mac, okay," Joe called back. "Come closer, will you, Baby?" he said to Teresa. She came closer to the bars, raised herself on the tip of her toes, and touched his lips.

"Good-by, Joe," she said.

"So long, Baby. It won't be long now."

"I will come again, soon."

"Better make it sooner than that," he kidded. But it was lost on her.

"I will try," she said.

As she passed the two policemen they stared at her trim figure, at the way her buttocks swelled against her skirt with each step. "I never saw a girl that small before who wasn't either too skinny and frail, or too fat and dumpy," ventured the rookie cop.

"Or with so many curves, eh," laughed the sergeant.

"Brother!" breathed the rookie. He walked toward the entrance, hoping to get another look at the girl.

CHAPTER FIFTEEN

SAM ROMA was worried. From the moment Teresa had reported her suspicions, he had begun to worry. And now, as he lay in his own bed, he felt his body grow damp with perspiration. His stomach felt as though it was tied up in a big soggy knot. His pajamas clung to his body in spite of the coolness of the night. How the hell could something like this happen to him? How could he explain to Cynthia? He laughed out loud. Explain to Cynthia? Was he going nuts, too? He simply couldn't explain it to her. There were some women that you just couldn't explain something like this to. Cynthia was one of them. And just when they had actually begun to plan for their marriage. At least Cynthia had begun to talk about it as though it weren't such a farfetched idea, after all.

Sam leaned over to the small table on the side of the bed. He fumbled for a cigarette, finally getting it into his mouth. He lit it with trembling hands. That damned girl. How could anyone be so stupid? Maybe she was wrong. How could anyone be so sure about something like that, so soon. He counted the days since he had first gone to her. He had to admit it was possible.

"Damn it to hell," he growled savagely. He leaned over to the ash-tray on the table and smothered the cigarette with an impulsive, impatient motion. Then he lay on his back with his head cupped under his hands.

What would happen when Joe got out? He had thought of it many times. But as quickly as it had entered his mind, just as quickly he had dismissed the thought. He would worry about it when the time came. But tonight, he could not easily overlook the inevitable. Joe would be out in several weeks. Then what?

"Good Lord!" he said hopelessly.

Anybody in his right mind would run from Joe, run from die girl. He hated her because of the trouble he was in; hated her because he could not resist her warm sensual body or her soft lips. He desired her, yet he hated her. Or did he hate her? He wondered how it would be if Cynthia wasn't in the picture.

Only tonight, in Teresa's bed, when she had whispered happily of her pregnancy he had grown cold and sick in the stomach. But her soft white arms had implored and caressed.

There was no denying her or himself. For a time, his lovemaking had been tender and gentle. He had felt a gush of sympathetic warmth for her, this girl who loved him so unselfishly. Especially at the final poignant moment when she had whispered: "Oh, my darling. How I love you. I love you. I love you."

But afterwards, with the reality and the severity of the situation pounding inside his head, he had gotten up abruptly and had left her. He could still see the surprised, confused look in her big eyes, even in the dim moonlight that swept the room. He had heard her call his name as he ran out of the front door.

He had too much to lose, if he ran away. When he married Cynthia, he would be set. Eventually, the quarry and the Cavallo holdings would become Cynthia's and his—if he could get her to marry him.

There were other deterrents. Where could he go? And more important—what would he do for dough? His perpetual wooing of Cynthia kept him constantly broke. At the moment, he had twelve bucks that he could call his own.

Deep within himself, and in spite of the arguments pro and con that were racing about in his mind, Sam Roma knew that he would not run—that he would stay to see this thing out. There was an inbred excitement that enveloped him, even now. Sam was no coward, for all of his faults. A time long ago, he might have been a gambler in a wild western town, or a pirate seeking and plundering gold-laden ships. He would have been an adventurer. There was something in his Sicilian blood that had made him fight Joe Carato, then take his woman. Even with the knowledge that it might have meant a revengeful death.

He fell asleep with his nerves tingling and with the some-what dubious knowledge that he would stick it out. He would play all the ends toward the center.

When Joe Carato finally came home the Road was engulfed by a hushed feeling of expectant violence. Usually, when Joe came home after a couple of days of cooling off in the county jail his house was open to all for a night of joyful merrymaking. On this cold, windy October day Joe was greeted only by Teresa. The men of the quarry were still at work, and the women peeped out from behind their shades. They did not know what to expect, unless it was to see Joe Carato go stomping up the road toward the quarry with murder in his heart.

They were somewhat surprised, when they saw him no more for the rest of the day. The men at the quarry kept glancing up the path expectantly. They watched as Sam Roma gave his orders, nervously smoking cigarette after cigarette. Where was Joe?

Giovanni was glad that Joe had not come. And he silently thanked God that the girl had been able to keep him away. Perhaps God, in his own way, had found a solution to this great problem. Angelo, the wine-maker, who worked close by, laid his pick down and straightened his back with a grunt. "Will we go to Joe's house tonight? I will bring wine."

"Who am I to say? When Joe comes, he will invite one and all, I am sure."

"Will he come?"

Giovanni shrugged his shoulders and continued digging.

"Will he kill Sam Roma?" asked Angelo persistently.

The others chimed in:

"Si, si! He must kill him!"

"*La vendetta! La vendetta!*"

"*Si,* Giovanni. It is only right." Angelo spoke his mind without fear, now that he knew the others were of his opinion.

"Quiet, you fools. If Joe does not come, it will be better for him." Giovanni was becoming angry.

"Sh!" someone whispered. "Sam is coming."

The men resumed their work. But out of the corners of their eyes, they watched as Sam strode down the path. He threw away his cigarette, and almost instantly lit another. The men received a partial gratification, at least, knowing that Sam wasn't enjoying himself on this hectic afternoon.

Teresa waited for Joe with a certain amount of misgiving. Life at the moment, was at its bleakest for her. Her eyes were red and swollen by tears. Sleep had not come easily to her, and the day had been spent anxiously peering out of the corner of the window facing the road.

Sam Roma had forsaken her. He had left her to face Joe alone, and for the first time in her life she was uncertain and afraid. In the past weeks, since Sam had stopped coming to her, she been alone in the empty house. Even Maria Colella had come only once. And the rest of the people of the quarry had left her alone to her fate. She had gone out only when necessary and had been frightened by the hostile glances she had received.

Certain now that she was pregnant she was confused and afraid. She was afraid of what Joe might do to her. But even more so, she was apprehensive and alarmed at what he might do to Sam Roma. She loved Sam still. She was certain of this. She knew it with every fiber of her being; she knew it because her body ached to be held in his arms. And she knew that no other man could now satisfy her needs.

The nights since he had stopped coming had been empty nightmares. The house had been filled with the ghost of the redhead. She had slept night after night with the lights of her bedroom burning brightly. She had heard him roaming about in the next room, and she had seen his ugly face leering down at her as she slept. She had awakened, screaming.

She had fallen asleep, crying and whimpering to the specter of the redhead, even more ugly in death. "I did not mean it. I did not want you to die," she cried.

And when she had fallen asleep again, he had gloated over her. He had laughed in unholy glee. The next morning she had wanted to run away from this house and its fearful memories. But she had nowhere to go. She had remained, and the nights were the same. Night after night, the redhead came to her, and be laughed and laughed.

Now at last, Joe stood in the doorway. For a moment, all of her fears left her. "Joe! Joe!" she laughed hysterically.

"Baby! Teresa, baby!" he called happily. He grabbed her and spun her about the room until she became dizzy. When he finally put her down, her back ached and she felt the nausea welling up in her stomach. He kissed her resoundingly on the lips, lifted her up again and started for the bedroom.

Terese squirmed out of his grasp and almost fell. "No, Joe. Please. I have supper ready."

Joe laughed uproariously. "Hey, that reminds me of the time I took you home. You remember we let the eggs get cold? Baby, the way I feel, supper can do the same thing." He started to grab for her again.

"No, Joe!" She squirmed away from him.

"Hey, what's the matter, Baby?" Joe stopped in his tracks, his arms out-stretched, his face twisted with uncertainty.

Now faced with the moment she had dreaded, Teresa spoke out defiantly. "I cannot sleep with you anymore, Joe," she said simply.

"This is no time for jokes, Baby," said Joe annoyed.

"I am not joking."

"I don't understand. What the hell's the matter with you, Teresa?" This was one of the few times that Joe had sworn at her, and Teresa's lips trembled.

"Joe," Teresa spoke softly and carefully, "I am pregnant."

Joe laughed until his body shook and the tears came from his eyes. "How do you like that? After all these years. And everybody thinks I can't have kids. Hey, wait until I tell Maria and Giovanni. Did you tell them yet?"

Teresa shook her head sadly. "Joe, it is not your baby."

Joe stopped laughing, the wind knocked out of him. His face darkened. "What?" he bellowed. "This is nothing to joke about, Teresa. I warn you." He towered over her ominously, his hands clenched into huge knotty fists.

"I do not joke with you, Joe." The fear in her made her eyes large, and she crouched against the wall. But her voice was steady and calm. And Joe was sure that she wasn't joking. In his mind, formed the question, incredible as it seemed. The redhead? He did not need to ask the question. Teresa's voice was a plaintive whine.

"Since the redhead died, I have been with another man. I have fallen in love with him."

"Who?" Joe whispered hoarsely. "Who?"

"I cannot tell you, Joe."

Joe's shoulders sagged, and he turned from her. He dragged himself to a chair and sat down heavily. His mind was in a turmoil. There was a time when he would have struck down a woman for less than this. But Teresa—she was so tiny, so frightened. And there was the baby. His or not, Joe Carato would never strike down a woman with a baby in her belly. Suddenly, he burst out with a shrill, mad laughter. What a damned fool! What a damned fool he was to think he could hold a beautiful woman such as this! He, so much older than she—such an ugly old man. He felt as old and as ugly as the redhead at the moment.

Teresa came before him. He stopped laughing suddenly, and looked at her. She showed no signs of her pregnancy. For a moment he had a small, tiny hope that perhaps she was wrong. "Are you sure, Baby?"

She nodded dumbly. "I have been to the doctor."

"But why, Teresa? Why?"

"I do not know. I only know that I love him."

"Who is it? Tell me who would come to take my woman."

"I cannot tell you, Joe. Maria has told me that you would kill him."

"Then they know. Everybody knows. They must be laughing at me. Teresa has put the horns on Joe Carato. Shouldn't I tear him apart with my bare hands? Shouldn't I, Teresa?" Joe shook his head.

"If you must kill someone, kill me. It is I who has wronged you."

"You really love him, eh, Teresa?"

She nodded.

"Then you'd better go to him."

"I cannot."

Joe raised his head, and the question was in his eyes.

"He has left me. He does not want me any longer."

"What?" Joe never could understand women. But this was preposterous. "And you want to stay here with me?"

"If you will have me."

Joe got up so suddenly and violently that Teresa retreated in fear. Joe's voice was bitter. "Put supper on the table while I go wash up."

Joe drank his coffee and leaned back in his chair. A loud burp escaped from his lips. Teresa looked anxiously at him. Not a word had been spoken by either throughout the entire meal. Joe had eaten slowly, pensively. He had been juggling the facts in his mind. He knew that he should have been crazy mad. He should have yelled and demanded to know who had done this thing to him. He should have stomped about the house, throwing and breaking things. It was the least that was expected of him by the citizens of the Quarry Road. He knew that they were all anxiously watching his house for some signs of violence. He would have to disappoint them.

How could he be so calm under the circumstances? Then he glanced at Teresa, looking on nervously, and he knew the reason why. In her eyes was the look of a small child, or it might have been a small dog who had gotten into some mischief, knew it and waited fearfully for her punishment. A small vein throbbed in her throat. Outside of that, she remained motionless, waiting for the worst.

As he ate, a thought had occurred to him. It had come to him suddenly and without any reasoning. And even then, when he should have been furious at the thought, he had remained strangely calm. Now, finally finished with his meal, he faced her squarely.

"Why did Sam Roma leave you?" he asked softly.

The girl was unprepared. "I do not know." she said simply. Then as the realization of what she had said came over her, her face paled and a look of fear distorted her features.

Now he knew what it was that had made him think of Sam Roma. He had seen that same look of fear in her eyes during the meal when they had heard Sam's car roar by on his way home from the quarry. He should have guessed sooner.

It was already getting dark outside. It became dark early this time of year. By now, all the men were home and enjoying a hot meal with their families. They were content, these men; content to be at home with their wives and their children. Across the way, he could see Giovanni and Maria moving about the house. They appeared nervous, glancing across at his house from time to time. He got up from the table.

"Where are you going?" she demanded anxiously.

"Where do you expect me to go?" he asked gently.

"You will not hurt him?"

"No, Teresa. I'm not going to hurt him. I'm not going to hurt a hair on his pretty head," Joe said sarcastically.

"Oh, I am so glad." The relief that flooded over her face made it shine with the gentle glow of a beautiful child.

"Teresa, how much do you love him?"

"Oh, Joe. I love him. I love him so much. He is the father of my baby."

"Would you want to marry him?"

The hope in her eyes was so obvious that Joe looked away. He could not bear that look wasted on the likes of Sam Roma. "Okay, Baby. Put on your wedding dress. We're going to find you a husband."

"Wedding dress?" she asked, puzzled.

"Put on your nicest dress." He laughed. "Well, go on," he said gruffly when she hesitated, not understanding the strange turn of events. "Don't you want to marry your Sam?" He took her by the shoulders and turned her about. Then he pushed her slowly toward the bedroom. He closed the door behind her and went back to the living room, smiling to himself. He wondered if he were suddenly going crazy. Was he doing wrong? At least Teresa would be happy. And Sam would be the most miserable person alive. He wanted to see him squirm when he had to face the Cavallo girl. That, he would like to see.

In a few moments, he heard Teresa calling through the closed door. He went to the door and opened it. The light in the room was out, but the light from the kitchen made it bright. Teresa stood by the bed, her skin pale. She was naked. Her firm breasts were in highlight and a shadow formed at her thighs. Joe's blood, cooled for so long, stirred and grew hot.

"This is the only way that I can thank you, Joe." There was no desire in her eyes. She simply intended to repay him for his kindness.

Joe started for her. His blood pounded at the sight of her desirable young body. She showed no signs of her pregnancy. The blood roared in his head. It made him dizzy; the feeling so strange after three months alone without his woman. He wanted her so much that he forgot the philanthropic mood he had worked himself into. He rushed to her and grabbed her roughly by the shoulders. His huge hands dug into her flesh until she cried out in pain. He threw her onto the bed savagely. She lay there, passive, looking up at him. There was no passion in her eyes. Only fright. He groaned and looked away.

"No, no, Baby! I should do it just to get even with that bastard. But I don't want you, knowing that you love him. You're his woman now. And Joe Carato respects another man's woman. You'd better hurry up and get dressed." He left the room, closing the door behind him.

CHAPTER SIXTEEN

CYNTHIA CAVALLO and Sam Roma attracted quite a bit of attention as they danced gracefully to the music in the dining room of the Pines Country Club. They floated easily around the room. Many of the diners paused to watch them. The men cast envious glances at Sam, but mostly their eyes were glued to Cynthia's undulating hips, as her tight skirt grew taut with each step, outlining the soft curves of her thighs and legs. The women looked at Sam Roma's handsome face and slim, athletic body. Then they looked at their own men and sighed resignedly.

When the number ended, Cynthia and Sam returned to their table. Sam lit cigarettes for both. They sat, not saying anything at all, waiting for their order to be brought in.

Cynthia was certain that something was bothering Sam. She recognized the sullen look that came over his features when he had something on his mind. He had had that same look about a month ago. He had gotten over it. Now, it was here again. She knew that the best thing to do at such times was simply to keep quiet. He had a nasty habit of snapping at her when he was in this mood. And although she was quite capable of putting him in his place, she certainly didn't want to start a scene here at the club. She would talk about it later.

And Sam was worried. He had plenty to worry about, now that Joe was out. Sooner or later, he would have to face him. At the moment, he was wishing that Joe had come to the quarry that day. Probably everything would have been straightened out by now. He might have been in the hospital, now, or even dead. But it would have been over with. This damned waiting was worse than facing ten Joe Caratos.

He would have to face Joe. It would probably be in the morning when Joe came to work. Sam had tried to get Joe fired, but Mr. Cavallo would not hear of it. Joe was worth three of the other men. He had been one of the first men to work for him when Mr. Cavallo himself had worked with the tools. This was long before Sam Roma had come upon the scene.

Sam felt sick to the stomach when one of the waiters came to the table. "A Mr. Carato wishes to speak to you, sir," he said. "He and his lady friend would like to join you at your table."

Sam looked at Cynthia. His face had turned white despite the deep tan.

"No, that won't be necessary. I'll see him out in the lobby," he told the waiter. He started to get up.

"Oh, Sam, let them join us," Cynthia broke in.

The waiter hesitated, looking at Sam.

"I'd rather speak to him outside, dear. You don't want them in here," argued Sam.

Cynthia was amused. She remembered the name now. It was Joe Carato who had fought with Sam. Apparently he had just gotten out of jail. "Oh, let them come in," she said gaily, enjoying the situation immensely. Sam glowered, but remained silent. She turned to the waiter. "Please tell them they may join us."

She recognized huge Joe Carato at once. She had seen him around the quarry many times. She had marveled at his bulging muscles, his powerful, ridged back soaked with perspiration. The girl who walked before him, she had never seen. She might have been his daughter, she looked so young. She was quite beautiful, and the cheap skirt and jacket failed to hide her well-rounded figure.

Sam had turned ashen-gray. He seemed to shrink deeper and deeper into his chair as they approached. Cynthia saw the girl looking fearfully at Sam. She had a moment of misgiving. Had she done right? There was an awkward pause as Joe and the girl stood by the table. Finally Cynthia spoke up. "Aren't you going to introduce your friends, Sam?"

Sam rose slowly, trying a weak smile. "Cynthia, I'd like you to meet Joe Carato. Joe, my fiancé, Cynthia Cavallo." He stood nervously by the table, wondering if the introductions had been done in the proper manner. He had caught himself in time and had not introduced the girl. He wasn't supposed to know her.

Joe nodded at Cynthia. "I know your father well. This is Miss Teresa Cardone." The girl nodded dumbly in the general direction of Cynthia. Joe held a chair for Teresa, then sat down.

"Won't you order?" asked Cynthia, always proper in her manners.

"No, thank you, Miss Cavallo," said Joe. "We came to see Sam. I believe he knows why."

She looked questioningly at Sam. He had sunk deeper into his chair, his handsome face lacking all expression. For the first time since she had known him, the arrogant look was missing from his face. She sensed that Joe was enjoying himself as much as she. The poor girl, however, appeared frightened out of her wits.

"Sam!" she spoke softly but sharply, "what is this all about?"

Sam ignored her. He turned to Joe. "Why did you come here, Joe? We could have settled this out at the quarry."

"Now, Sam," Joe's voice was oily, "don't you think Miss Cavallo has a right to know what's going on? After all, it does concern her in a way."

There was a dull thrill of excitement that welled inside Cynthia. And she was fearful of what she was about to find out. She did not like the way the girl's eyes remained glued to Sam's face. "Will someone please tell me what this is all about?" she begged. She looked at Joe's bland face; at Sam's face, grim, and frowning mad; at Teresa who could not keep her eyes from Sam Roma.

Finally, Joe Carato spoke up.

"Miss Cavallo, I came here to right a great wrong. I want no trouble with Sam. I only want him to marry this poor girl. You see, she's in trouble. In very bad trouble."

The impact of Joe's statement hit Cynthia with the force of a giant sledge, and the excitement drained out of her body and left her weak. She looked at the girl opposite her with new interest. Now that she knew the reason for their coming, she felt that she had known it all along. She looked at Sam. He appeared to be looking to the floor for a means of escape.

"I'm sure you have an explanation, Sam," she said. Her voice had an edge of forced assurance.

"If you think you can force me into this," Sam snarled at Joe.

"Want to step outside and see if I can or not?" asked Joe. He did not hold back now. "You stole into my house like a cheap thief while I was in jail. You took my woman. And now you're trying to tell me that I can't make you marry her, and give her baby a name. Mister, you're getting off easy."

They had all been talking in an undertone and had attracted no attention from the other tables. But now, Joe's voice had begun to rise. Some of the nearby diners looked up.

"I'm sure Sam will do what is right, Mr. Carato," said Cynthia. She rose from the table. There was an icy glint in her blue eyes. "Please take me home, Sam."

Joe and Sam rose. Teresa remained seated, a passive, stupid glare in her eyes. Cynthia walked away from the table. Sam followed her. To all outward appearances, there was nothing in the world wrong with these two.

They drove away from the club, without a word being spoken by either. The night was cool, almost cold as it swirled through the open windows of the car. It cleared Sam's brain, and for the past several minutes, he had been busy making up excuses. He would have to tell Cynthia something. And it had better be good. He had it! It was all her fault. How long could a guy be kept on the string. He was only human. He would tell Cynthia that the girl had forced her attentions on him; that he had had practically no alternative. He'd make it good.

Soon they came to the main highway. Cynthia's home was several miles north. He was surprised when she directed him to drive south. He obeyed without a word, and soon they were out of the town limits. He kept on driving, not knowing their destination, if there was any. Nor did he care. The girl, sitting tight against the opposite side of the car, said nothing.

They had driven about twenty miles through open country. A brilliantly lighted sign, in the shape of a cottage, sprang up before them in the distance. *Jerry's Cottage Motel* was spelled out in large, red neon signs. The signs went on and off, but the light that framed the shape of the cottage remained lit.

"Turn in at the motel," whispered Cynthia huskily. Sam swallowed hard, not daring to believe what he heard. He turned the car smoothly into the driveway.

"Please get a cabin." For the first time since leaving the club, Sam looked at her. "Well, don't you want to?" she asked bitterly when she saw the surprised look in his face.

He parked the car, left it and went into the office. A fat, sleepy man took his money and made him sign the register. Sam saw a Mr. and Mrs. Smith already entered, so he wrote Mr. and Mrs. Brown. The man gave him a key. "Number Seven," he said. "Last cabin on this side." He sat down heavily into a rocking chair, grunted as he leaned over to pick a newspaper from the floor, then lost interest in Sam Roma.

Sam hurried back to the car and got in. He drove slowly between the two rows of cabins, pulled around the last one and braked the car. He turned to Cynthia, sitting straight in her seat and looking straight ahead.

"Okay, now tell me what this is all about."

"Is this our cabin?"

"Yeah."

She got out of the car without answering. She went to the entrance of Number Seven and tried the door. It was locked. Sam followed her to the door. He looked furtively about. Several of the cabins were lit up with cars parked in front of them. Sam's car was well out of sight around the corner. Another car pulled in to the driveway and stopped in front of the office. He opened the door quickly and let Cynthia in. Then he entered. He closed the door behind him and switched on the light.

Cynthia looked around. She pulled down a blind, opened a door and looked into a cubby-hole containing the toilet, sink and a shower. Somewhere, a radio began to play softly. Behind another door was the only closet. She took a clothes hanger and hung it on the door knob. Then, before the unbelieving eyes of Sam Roma, she began to strip. She hung her coat and dress carefully in the closet. She took off her slip and laid it over a chair. Sam's temples began to drum as the blood pounded in his veins.

She reached behind her and unclasped her brassiere. For the first time, she looked at him; saw his eyes widen in wonder as her proud breasts came free. She lay the brassiere beside the slip. Her long full body gleamed under the light, her breasts thrusting out, the tiny virginal brown tips already hard. They hung heavily as she leaned over and slipped the wispy black panties over her waist and down over long smooth legs. She stood before him in all her proud nakedness.

"Well," she said, "isn't this what you've wanted all along."

Sam sprang across the room. Her body arched to meet his. His clothing bruised her skin, but she turned up her mouth to him, and he kissed her hard. He had never found her mouth as soft and warm and willing.

"Your clothing is hurting me," she whispered, catching her breath.

For the life of him, he could not understand what had come over Cynthia. He didn't stop to question her actions. He threw his clothes in a desperate heap about him. He went swiftly to her as she lay on the bed. She stared wide-eyed.

For a moment, she tensed with fright. His mouth found hers again in a long, tender kiss. All the pent-up emotions that she had kept from him, saved for their wedding night, welled up in her. Her body relaxed and grew soft. A tiny groan escaped her....

From a distance, she heard Sam pleading forgiveness for her pain. But now, there was no longer pain. There had never been pain. There was only an exquisite feeling of weakness; of a languor never before experienced until now. Sam's arms were wrapped under her back. Her arms held his head down to her breast. She had never felt such soul-searching exhaustion.

"Kiss me," she whispered.

He found her lips, now swollen, and they lay in that position for several minutes. Then, quite suddenly, as though her strength had suddenly returned to her, she pushed him from her and sat up.

"You forgot to turn off the light," she said. Her tone was impersonal. He might have been a stranger. He had a glimpse of her back, smoothly gleaming from the slight perspiration. A series of red welts remained where the sheets on the bed had gathered into ridges and marked her body. Then she disappeared into the bathroom. He felt the sting as his back touched the sheets. He had not felt her nails until now.

The shower went on in the other room, and he heard her splashing. He still couldn't figure out what had happened to Cynthia. He hadn't had much time to think about it, actually. He grinned. Things had certainly taken an amazing turn. Cynthia had claimed him for her own. They would get married now, and to hell with Joe Carato and the girl. He grinned again. He found it hard to believe that Cynthia could be such a passionate woman.

The shower was turned off, and a cloud of steam billowed out as Cynthia opened the door and came into the room. She was rubbing her body vigorously with a towel, leaving it a blushing pink as the blood rushed to the surface of her smooth skin. Her hair was still dry. She had been careful not to wet it. Once dried, she began to dress.

"Please get dressed and let's get out of this place," she said.

"Let's not go yet," he begged.

"We must." There was signs of nervousness about her now. "I hate this place."

He got out of the bed and went to her. He wanted to hold her, to tell her that he loved her more than ever. He wanted to get her back to the bed. When he tried to take her in his arms, she impatiently twisted out of his grasp.

"Please, Sam!"

He let her alone, then, and began to dress.

Cynthia covered her stately nakedness slowly, carefully. He watched her apprehensively. Her mood had changed.

He shut the light as they left the cabin. He wondered whether he should bring the key back to the office, decided against it, and left it in the lock. They got into the car. He backed up into the areaway, made a turn and pulled out of the driveway into the highway. He drove slowly in the direction of her home. It was chilly in the car. The girl shivered until the car warmed up.

"Well, what do we do now?" asked Sam.

"What do you mean?"

"We'll have to get married—now."

"Why?" Her voice was casual.

"Why?" he echoed. "I love you. After what happened, I insist on it."

"I'm afraid that's impossible, Sam. I'd respect you more as a man, if you married that poor girl." Her voice was calm.

Sam's voice rose perceptibly. "I couldn't marry her. I love you. It's your fault, in a way. I've begged you a hundred times to marry me. Now that this has finally happened between us, you want to shut me out. Why the cabin, then? It would have been better all around, if we hadn't gone."

The girl hesitated for a moment. She looked out at the darkness whirling by until Sam thought she was ignoring him. She finally spoke. "I don't know what made me do it, Sam. Maybe it was a woman's vanity. You don't know how angry and bitter I was the moment I heard of you and that girl. I wanted to hurt you, to show you how it could have been if you had only been a little more patient. I wanted to show you what you were missing when I left you. I intended to cut you off, afterwards—stop seeing you."

"Oh, no!" Sam groaned.

"You needn't worry, Sam." Cynthia sounded sad. "I'm afraid my little scheme has back-fired. I never thought it could be like that—that a man's body could mean so much to a woman."

"Well, then. Marry me."

"I don't know, Sam. I'm all confused. I know that I want you now, more than ever. I would marry you tonight. But there's the baby. If it was only that girl, I would never give you up."

"Look, Cynthia. Let me worry about that. Let's go some-where and get married, tonight. Then I'll worry about the baby when it's born."

"Do you think Joe Carato would let you get away with it? I think not. No, I won't have it any other way. You'll have to marry that girl."

"And us?"

"Sam." The girl's voice was a bare whisper. "Marry the girl, and I promise to see you again."

"You mean—the cabin and all?"

"Yes."

"And if I don't marry her?"

"Then I shall never see you again. Don't you see, Sam. I could never marry you, knowing that you have a bastard child around. It would always come between us. Marry the girl and give the baby a name. After it's born, you can get a divorce. Then I would marry you without hesitation."

They drove silently for several miles. Sam went over Cynthia's proposition. It sounded feasible enough. It seemed to solve every-thing. And with Cynthia thrown in as an extra bonus. Not bad. He did not want to appear too happy about the whole thing, however.

"I don't know," he said doubtfully.

"Is the choice so hard to make?" Sam noted a tinge of sar-casm in her voice. "It's just like asking a child if she wants all the playthings or none."

"But I don't love her." This was Sam's last resort, his last argu-ment. If Cynthia was testing him, this was the right thing to say.

"She is a beautiful woman. Although she did appear a little stupid."

"I could never love her. I'm crazy about you. You know that, Cynthia."

"Well then. It should be easier than I'd expected. You can live with her on a strict platonic basis. Just for appearance's sake, until the baby comes."

"And then—?"

"I told you. You get a divorce and we can get married."

"That's the only way you'll have it?"

"Yes, Sam. I'm afraid that it is the only way."

There was nothing more to argue about. Sam knew she had made up her mind. He knew her well enough to realize that he couldn't change it for her.

Sam braked the car for a red light at an intersection. Cynthia stole a glance at his face. He was frowning thoughtfully. The car pulled away smoothly. They were silent all the way to her home.

The Cavallo home was a new contemporary ranch type, with a long low roof and stone retaining walls that held the sloping grounds in place. A driveway led to a two-car garage built into the basement of the house. Cynthia's car was parked outside the garage. A large curved picture window faced the driveway, and dim lights were visible inside the house.

"Your people are still up," said Sam, after pulling into the driveway. He turned off the ignition key and doused the headlights.

"It's only ten-thirty," said Cynthia.

Sam was overly satisfied at the way things had turned out. As Cynthia had pointed out—It was really very simple. Either he took everything or nothing. No halfway measures for her. And he knew that she meant every word; that she would keep her promise. What the hell, if that was the way she wanted it, why not? He thought of the girl, Teresa. She wasn't hard to take. And Cynthia had been a pleasant surprise.

"Cynthia," he whispered.

"Yes, Sam."

"You're sure this is the way you want it?"

"Yes, Sam. That's the way I want it."

"And you'll continue seeing me?"

"I said I would." She had been sitting against the door on her side of the car. Now, she leaned over so that her bosom pushed hard against Sam's shoulder. Her long blonde hair tickled his face as he received her kiss. "There'll be other nights like this, Sam. I promise."

Sam started to grab her. But she pulled away. "Good night, Sam," she said. "I'm tired.' She opened her door and stepped out. She came around to his side. "Good night, Sam." She leaned into the car and kissed him again. "You'll take care of everything?"

Sam nodded. "I'll call you tomorrow?"

"No, Sam. Don't call me until you've taken care of that girl."

"That's the way you want it?"

She nodded. "Good night, Sam." She turned and walked away toward the house. Sam watched as she let herself in. Then, he backed out of the driveway. He looked longingly at the new stone house; at the row of individually styled singles that housed the upper crust of the town. He pressed hard on the accelerator and roared out of the wide, curving street.

CHAPTER SEVENTEEN

SO IT WAS that Sam Roma married Teresa and brought her to his apartment. Joe Carato was happy for the girl. For himself, he was not so happy. He missed her. There was no mistaking the symptoms of his loneliness; the empty, voiceless house; his clothing, dirty and ragged, and the cold meals; the bed, empty and lifeless. He missed her more now, than he had when in jail. In jail, he had his hopes to comfort him. Now there was no hope. Teresa was too happy with Sam. There could be no hope for Joe Carato.

Giovanni told him over and over again, that it was as it should be. The people of the quarry consoled him—when he would listen. He had done the proper thing. He would soon find a nice girl, they told him. Mrs. Giambra let it be known in no uncertain terms that she was available. She invited him to supper several times. Joe refused.

At the quarry, there was, to all outward appearances, no animosity between Joe and Sam Roma. They never discussed Teresa. And the work went smoothly. The men worked as hard as ever, Joe setting the example. The winter was a mild one, and the men lost little time because of the weather. They were content. There was no reason why things should not be as pleasant as they were—now that the girl was gone.

Teresa was blissfully happy in her new role as Mrs. Roma. Slim and childlike, in the early part of her pregnancy, she showered Sam with her love and affection. She could not do enough for him. Sam began to look forward to the hot meals, he knew would be waiting for him. His clothes were always clean and freshly laundered. And she had changed the apartment into a cozy, well-kept home. She made no demands on him, and never once mentioned Joe Carato, to even ask how he was. And Sam was more content than he had anticipated.

From the first night together in the apartment, he had forgotten Cynthia's appeal. How could it be possible to live with this vibrant, wholesome woman on a strict platonic basis? She was never demanding in their love-making. But there was no need to demand it. Sam Roma seemed never to get enough of her. And she was incapable of denying herself to him. She gave of herself so completely that at times she was completely exhausted and fell asleep almost immediately.

Sam continued seeing Cynthia, however. It was part of the bargain, and he demanded it of her. He usually had to get in touch with her several times before she came. And then, only when she felt that she could stand the craving for him no longer. Then she would meet him secretly, and they would drive to the motel where she exhausted her pent-up passion. These meetings were short, turbulent and animal like. Cynthia stripped off the cloak of coolness and aloofness, to become a panting, insatiable woman. At these times, Sam came away with his shoulders and back ripped and bleeding where she had clawed him. She would dress swiftly as though afraid to let him feast on her body, urging him to dress quickly and leave. He would drive her to a spot, not far from the motel where she usually left her car, and she would drive off by herself. Never, under any circumstances, would she allow herself to be seen in his company. As far as anyone knew, they had broken completely.

Toward the end, when Teresa's body became swollen and refused to awaken at his touch, when she wished only to lie near him and feel his body warmth and tender caresses, Sam began to brood. He demanded that Cynthia see him more often. He begged to spend a night with her. But to no avail. She would see him only when she felt the need for him. His arguments became more violent, and his demands more insistant. After one such argument, she refused to see him for two weeks. And only after he threatened to make a scene at her home, did she consent to see him.

She met him, and, once more, her body betrayed her. Afterwards, lying exhausted, and somewhat bitter that she had given in to him, she started to get out of the bed. Sam. held on to her good-naturedly. With a wild cry she turned on him. Sam was caught unawares. A red gash appeared along his arm as he tried to ward off her flashing nails. He caught her in a bear-hug before she could do more damage.

"Let me go, Sam," she whispered through clenched teeth. "Let me go or I'll scream my head off."

"What the hell's the matter with you, Cynthia? Have you gone crazy or something?" He held on to her.

"You think you can treat me like a whore? You would like me to be at your disposal any time you want me, wouldn't you? Well, I won't be." She had relaxed against him, her arms pinioned against her side. "Now, let me go."

Sam had never heard her use that word before. When the occasion for its use had come up, she had used the word, prostitute, instead. It struck him funny. He started to laugh. "You're starting to talk like one, dear," he said.

Instantly, she became a furious, clawing tigress. Her teeth sank into the fleshy part of his arm. Her nails made short ragged gouges on his face and chest.

Sam was rapidly becoming a mass of blood. It was impossible to ward off her vicious thrusts. Sam finally managed to straddle her; to force her arms along her side. She struggled to free herself.

"I hate you! I hate you!" she cried. She got her right arm free and ripped his chest in an effort to get at his eyes. The pain made Sam scream. His heavy calloused hand came down in an arc, and there was a resounding clap, as he slapped her hard across the face.

The fight went out of her. She lay limp, looking with growing horror at his blood-flaked body, actually seeing it for the first time. A tiny trickle of blood appeared on her lips from a small gash inside her mouth. Sam grew frightened. He tore a corner of the sheet and went into the bathroom. He soaked it and hurried out. He opened her mouth, gently, and pressed the cloth against the cut. Her eyes were wide with wonder and fear, as she allowed him to treat her lip.

When the bleeding had finally stopped, he leaned over her and kissed her gently. With an anguished cry, she drew him down to her. "Oh, Sam, Sam!" she cried. He held her as her tears fell against some of the scratches on his arm and made it burn. Her crying turned to sobs, and finally she fell asleep. He was content to lay there and hold her in his arm.

He had to wake her several hours later. She could have slept right through. "It's after twelve, dear," he said. "Your people might start worrying about you."

She opened her eyes slowly, not realizing where she was. Sam was already dressed. He had taken a shower a half hour before. Some of his scratches itched, and he scratched the spots carefully.

He helped her out of the bed, and she began to dress slowly, without taking a shower. Sam watched her anxiously. They left the cabin and drove silently until Sam pulled the car up behind hers.

"Cynthia!" He tried to take her in his arms. She remained cool and unresponsive.

"Please Cynthia, honey. Please forgive me," Sam begged.

"I forgive you," she said coolly.

"You know I didn't mean to hurt you. I wouldn't hurt you for the world." She was silent. "When you said you hated me, I lost my head. You do love me, don't you?"

"Yes, I love you, Sam." Her tongue licked the tiny cut in her mouth, and she winced.

"Does it hurt?" he asked.

"A little."

"Oh, baby, I'm so sorry."

"Please forget it, Sam."

"When will I see you again, Cynthia?" Sam's voice was a pleading, whipped whisper.

"I don't know, Sam. I will call you."

"Please don't keep me waiting. I don't know what I'll do, if I don't see you soon."

Cynthia's voice was soft, and her body relaxed in his arms. "I'll call you soon. I promise."

When he kissed her, she responded, and her lips became warm and soft. "I'll wait for you, then." He had felt the warmth of her kiss, and his heart felt lighter. He got out of the car and opened her door. She got out, her long legs forcing her skirt high above her knees. He held her hand until she was standing close to him. The cold chill of the night made her shiver, and he saw a tenderness in her eyes that he had not seen in a long time. He kissed her again. She strained against him until he could feel the curves of her body through their coats. He finally pulled away. He led her to her car and watched as she drove off.

Cynthia loved Sam.

In her car, she stared ahead, unseeing. The miles flew by without her realizing it. For her mind was back in the cabin, back with Sam and his love.

At the moment that Sam had slapped her, something had happened to her. To see Sam so remorseful and begging for forgiveness, had created a feeling, utterly strange to her. It had formed a gnawing doubt in herself. She had begun to wonder if indeed she were a woman with a woman's feelings. Up till now, she had been content with satisfying her sexual desires. Actually, she had used Sam. And Sam had shown tonight that he wanted her as a woman, and not as a piece of flesh. When he had begged her for forgiveness, almost in tears; for the first time in her life, she had understood him. In spite of his tough, sullen exterior, he was like a little boy. And he needed her.

And she needed him. She knew that now. Their moments together were both gratifying and complete. She knew now that Sam could be tender and sweet afterwards, if only she would let him. She felt a misgiving now that she had never felt before. It was she who had caused Sam all this trouble. He had been right, indirectly, she was responsible for letting him wait, dangling on a string, until he had been driven into the arms of that girl.

She came to a final conclusion as she drove into the driveway of her home. She would wait for Sam. She would go to him, be a wife to him. She would love him for himself—and not for herself.

Later, in her bed, she wept uncontrollably and unashamed. If only it were she, living with Sam. If only her body were swollen and misshapen with Sam's baby. "If only—if only it were me," she cried bitterly. Her pillow was wet with her tears when she turned it over and finally fell asleep.

CHAPTER EIGHTEEN

JOE CARATO ate with a great appetite. It had been so long since he had eaten a meal such as this. And he made the most of it, enjoying every morsel as though it was to be his last. Giovanni and Maria looked on with great satisfaction. They had invited him over for supper several times. Until now, he had refused.

It was a cool, clear Sunday afternoon, and the Colella family was still dressed in all it's Sunday finery. They made an impressive sight around the big, round table. The children were noisy but well behaved. Giovanni, sitting at the head of the table, would have it no other way. A dark look from him was enough to scare the devilment out of any one of the children.

By now the meal was nearly over. Maria sat next to her husband, finally managing to get a chance to eat.

"Giovanni, you are the luckiest man in the world," said Joe, smacking his lips. "To have a wife like Maria and a family like this is something to be proud of."

Giovanni grinned. "Joe, my friend, have more wine. I like the way you talk when you are drunk." He filled Joe's glass again.

"You know I never meant anything more in my life," Joe insisted. "And it's not the wine that makes me say it."

The aroma of roast chicken and meat-ball and sausage gravy still permeated the room. It was a heart-warming and satisfying aroma. "This supper was fit for a king," Joe continued.

"Do you think it is like this always?" Giovanni winked at Joe. "Ah, no, my friend. It is only today that we eat so well. It is only because you have come, that Maria cooks such a good meal."

Maria pushed Giovanni affectionately. She knew that he was kidding her, as did Joe. Maria was easily the best cook in the tiny community. "Someday, you will come home and not find anything to eat," she said. "Then, I would like to hear you."

The smaller children had finished eating and had left the table after asking the father's permission. The twelve-year-old was clearing the table. A pot of coffee was beginning to boil, lending a new aroma to the room.

"What do you think, Joe?" said Giovanni absently. "We saw Teresa in church today. She was by herself." He felt the kick under the table and knew that he had done wrong.

Joe looked up sharply. "Is she well?" he asked, trying to keep his voice under control.

Maria looked at Joe. "She is fine, Joe. She has grown very large. It will be a big baby."

Giovanni saw the interest that came into his daughter's eyes. "We will not need you here any longer," he said. The girl left hurriedly. "My little girl is impatient to learn," he said to Joe.

"Sam Roma must be treating her well. She seems very happy, Joe," said Maria.

"I'm glad." Joe sighed deeply, took another drink of wine.

Maria looked sadly and shook her head. She knew it was a sore subject with Joe. "You miss her, eh, Joe?"

"Maria, I would do anything if she would come back to me. I would even raise Sam's kid as my own."

Maria set cups and saucers and teaspoons on the table. She held the pot with a corner of her apron as she poured coffee. Then she placed a sugar bowl and cream pitcher on the table and sat down.

"Hey, Joe," said Giovanni, "what is the matter with Mrs. Giambra? She has such a good business. You would do well to take her as your woman. She is willing."

Maria sniffed. "You are better off as you are, Joe."

"You're right, Maria. That woman with her tongue would drive me to drink. I'm afraid there'll be no other for me."

"You will find another, Joe. There are many women in the world," said Maria.

"Perhaps, when I'm tired of Maria, I will let you have her," Giovanni grinned. He took the light blow on his shoulder laughingly.

"And to think that you go to church," chided Maria.

"That is it, Joe. You must come to church with us and pray. The Virgin Mother will help you."

"You know I don't go to church, Giovanni. It's been a long time since I went to one."

"There is nothing like prayer," said Maria.

"Then you pray for me, Maria."

"I will do it."

"You'll have to pray very hard. Because I won't be satisfied with anyone but Teresa."

"Don't worry, my friend," said Giovanni, "I will make all my little ones pray for you. The Virgin Mother listens to little ones. They will make a strong prayer for you."

"Okay, Giovanni. I will wait." Joe was in better spirits now. He called the twelve-year-old from the other room. She came to him, and he handed her a dollar bill. "Here, go to Mrs. Giambra and get ice cream for all the children. I will need them on my side."

The third of May was a day never to be forgotten at the quarry. It was a balmy, pleasantly warm day. For the past week, the men had begun to discard their heavy winter work clothes in favor of sweaters and sweatshirts. Already, they had begun to work up a sweat, and they gloried in the knowledge that they had before them the long period of Spring and Summer and Autumn. The winter was behind them.

Tiny shoots of grass had begun to push out of any little crevice that had imprisoned a bit of the earth. It made the ugly gray of the shattered rock seem bedecked in green ribbons.

Joe Carato looked anxiously up at the top of the crater. And the men looked anxiously at Joe. It was almost ten o'clock and Sam Roma had not arrived. Now, they were beginning to wonder if they had done right in starting to work. Maybe Sam would be angry, and he would not pay them for the two hours they had already put in. Suppose they worked all day, and Sam did not come all day. Would he believe that they had worked, that they had earned a good day's wages? Suppose he would not pay them for all day? So they looked at Joe, who was their spokesman in such matters.

But Joe was not concerned with this. If Sam had not shown up for work, there could be only one reason. Teresa was having her baby.

Giovanni sidled up to Joe. "What do you think, Joe?" Fine beads of perspiration had popped out on forehead.

"What do you mean, Giovanni?"

"The men are worried, Joe. They do not know if they do right in working without Sam."

"Tell them to go home, then. I can't tell them what to do."

"I will stay if you stay," said Giovanni.

Joe turned to the men. "Listen. I don't know what to say. I can't tell you to stay or go home. I'm staying."

"Then we will stay," chorused several of the men. They fell back to work.

"Why do you worry, Joe?" asked Giovanni. "You think maybe Teresa will have her baby today?"

"Yes, Giovanni."

"Maria said that it will be today or tomorrow. She knows."

"Sh. Be quiet, Giovanni. I think I hear Sam's car." The men began working feverishly, wanting to impress Sam with the work they had done. When they saw his car coming right down into the pit on the ramp used only by the trucks, they felt sure that they were in for it. Sam never drove his car into the hole. He was angry with them for sure.

Sam bounded out of the car, amid the dust it had churned up. He rushed over to Joe Carato, and he fairly trembled with rage. "You son of a bitch!" he screamed. "You dirty son of a bitch!"

Sam Roma had finally gone mad, summerized the men. To talk to Joe Carato like this—was indeed madness. Had he already forgotten the last beating at Joe's hands? They watched silently and prayed that Joe would be kind.

Joe did nothing but stare. He stood still like a huge stone statue, his pick poised in mid-air and stared at Sam Roma. Sam rushed up to Joe and snatched the pick out of his hands. He raised it high over his head, and there was no doubting his intentions. There was murder in his eyes. The men gasped.

But now, Joe moved and with amazing speed for his size. Before Sam could start his downward swing, Joe grabbed the pick and yanked down and behind Sam. It came out of his hands quite easily, Sam falling back into a sitting position. The men grouped around them.

"Now, tell me what the hell is wrong," said Joe calmly.

But Sam sat, his head buried in his hands and he shook with frustrated rage. The men smiled at each other. To see Sam in this position was truly amusing. Joe knelt down beside Sam.

Suddenly, he felt sorry for him. But uppermost in his mind, was a tiny fear. Something had happened to Teresa.

"Sam, what's wrong? For God's sake, did something happen to Teresa?"

Sam looked at him. He had stopped shaking, but his eyes were still blazing with fury. "I'll kill you for this, Joe. I'll kill you for what you did to me."

"Will you try to make sense? Where's Teresa? Did she have her baby?"

"Yeah, she had her baby," Sam said bitterly.

"So why do you have it in for me," Joe asked.

"You made me marry her, you bastard. You ruined it for Cynthia and me." Sam began to talk rationally. He got up, brushed himself off. "All right, you guys. Get back to work." The men scurried back to work. All except Joe. He had to get things straightened out.

"All right, Sam. What's wrong? You did right by Teresa. You got her in trouble."

"I did like hell." He said it loudly so that all the men heard.

"What do you mean, Sam? Everybody knows you did it." Joe was getting angry.

"Joe, if that baby ain't the redhead's baby, I'll eat every rock in this damned lousy quarry."

"The redhead!" Joe's mouth gaped, his lower lip hanging slack. "What the hell are you talking about?"

Sam was serious, in dead earnest, trying to convince Joe. "I swear, Joe. I never saw a kid look so much like the father. Red hair, eyes that look right through you. The kid scared the daylights out of me. I thought I was seeing the redhead's ghost."

"Well what do you know?" Joe burst out laughing. He shouted at the men. "How do you like that redhead?" Then to

Sam, "You're sure, Sam? You're not trying to pull something over on that girl?"

"Go see for yourself. And Joe—" he paused for effect—"I'm not taking responsibility for that kid or Teresa, either. I'm getting an annullment as soon as I can."

"Look, Sam. If that kid ain't yours, I'll take them both off your hands. Don't worry about that."

"I said go see for yourself," Sam said gruffly.

Joe started running up the ramp. Sam looked at the men. They had all stopped working. "All right, get back to work," Sam shouted. But Sam was grinning. They went back to work. They were all grinning, too. It was a beautiful day. It was a day fit for a miracle.

Joe Carato rushed to the hospital as though his life depended on it. But when he got there, he had to wait around until he felt like pushing his fist through a wall. The nurses who passed him in stiff, crackling uniforms, thought for certain, that here was another husband waiting and suffering, while his wife brought him forth an heir. Though heaven knows, there wasn't much to inherit, from the looks of him.

He was finally allowed to see the baby. Through a big glass partition, he looked into a room full of basinets. Three held tiny babies, wrapped carefully and laying helpless. Two were asleep. The third was crying lustily. His crib shook precariously as his little hands punched the air in snort jerky motions. The other babies winced in their sleep at the sound of the crying.

Then, as if sensing Joe's presence, the baby stopped crying, and it seemed to stare deep into his very soul. And Joe looked at the orange-red hair and back at the eyes. And he saw Redhead. The baby squinted at him, and it was Redhead all over again. Just as he used to squint in the sunlight, like a wild animal coming out of its cave after a long winter's hibernation.

Then the baby smiled at him. He had Teresa's smile, Joe thought. He would be a handsome boy. Joe stared to grin. "I'll be damned," he said. "I'll be damned to hell!" He burst out laughing. And the baby laughed with him.

When he finally saw Teresa, she had just awakened. She lay pale and calm in the hospital bed. There were three other beds in the room, but they were empty. Two showed signs of having been slept in.

"Teresa, baby," he said. "You're looking swell." He bent over and kissed her on the forehead.

"Hello, Joe," she said softly. "Did you see the baby?"

"Yeah, it's a fine baby."

"Sam saw it. He was very angry."

"I know. He was angry with me, too." Joe grinned. "He wanted to fight me because he said I forced him to marry you."

"But what is wrong? I do not understand." She sounded genuinely puzzled.

"Did you see the baby?" Sam asked.

"Yes."

"It doesn't look like Sam, does it?" Joe spoke patiently.

"No."

"It looks like Redhead. Like Jake Malancuni, doesn't it, Teresa?"

"Yes." Her voice was small and pitiful. "But why should Sam be angry because it does not look like him?"

"Teresa, baby, listen to me. Did you—?" Joe did not quite know how to express himself. "Did you and the redhead—?"

"Oh—" Teresa's eyes grew wide as she finally began to understand. She seemed about to cry. "Oh, Joe," she whispered plaintively. "I did not mean to trick Sam. I did not know. I am so sorry."

"It's all right, Baby."

"But Sam is so angry with me."

"Sam wants to divorce you. He knows that the baby is not his. It is the redhead's, isn't it?"

"Yes, I think so. It could be. Oh, I don't know." Her face had turned a healthy pink in her confusion. "Oh, Joe," she whimpered. "What will I do? If Sam does not want me, where can I go with the baby?"

"Don't worry, Baby. You come right back home with me."

"You will take me back?"

"Yes."

"And the baby, too?"

"Sure. I said I would. Even if you still love Sam," said Joe, wistfully.

"Oh, Joe." Teresa was in tears. "I will be good to you. I will forget Sam. It will be only you and the Dally from now on. I promise you."

"I guess the redhead will be happy, where-ever he is," said Joe.

"We must forget him, too, Joe."

"Yeah, Baby. Everytime I look at the baby, I'll forget about the redhead," he answered with good-natured sarcasm. He knew it was lost on her. She was such a stupid girl, this woman of his.

THE END

www.ingramcontent.com/pod-product-compliance
Lightning Source LLC
Chambersburg PA
CBHW020915180626
46816CB00007BA/2408